Forever Yours

Peacock Publishing Ltd

1997

Forever Yours

Published by Peacock Publishing Ltd
3, St. Mary's Street
Worcester WR1 1HA, England

ISBN 0-9525404-8-7

Cover design: Excalibur Graphics 1997

British Library cataloguing-in-print data has been applied for.

Typeset in New Century Schoolbook 10pt

Printed in Malta by Interprint Ltd

CHAPTER 1

"You know, you're gorgeous, Lorne," Lance said softly. His narrow lips were twisted into a smile; his thin, quirky eyebrows raised in admiration.

"Thanks." He must have picked up the irritation in her tone. At that moment, a compliment from Lance was the last thing she wanted. "Can we get on now? There's something I need to check."

Lorne flicked back her thick, blonde hair, bleached white by the sun. She knew what Lance was imagining. Her falling into his arms. But she didn't want him. And if what she'd found out today was true, then he had no chance.

She crossed her smooth, golden-brown legs and glanced at him sharply. He'd better not make another comment about them. *Never-ending* was one of his favourites. She'd gone along with his smarminess a few months ago when she was horribly lonely. But she'd stopped herself being taken in - and now she was glad.

The office was unbearably hot. At twelve, the Canarians went home to lunch and then their siesta. Doubtless that was what Lance had in mind by the look on his face. For her and himself. Together. But she wasn't interested.

"Damn this heat," he growled, loosening his tie. "Okay.

What do you want? Fire away, Lorne. The sooner we get home, the better." His moodiness was showing again. It always did when someone upset him. In this case, her.

She could feel tiny beads of perspiration bursting their salt on her lips. The typed letters on the architect's plans spread out on the desk, jigged up and down in front of her eyes; the breeze off the sea wasn't making the slightest difference to this unbearably hot morning. And Lance was still staring at her legs. She could have had him for sexual harassment a number of times.

"Come on, Lorne." Lance didn't pull his punches. His remarks could be taken however a girl wanted, but Lorne wasn't having any. She uncrossed her legs deliberately.

She was a business woman and independent. She did not rely on him for work. He could take the gesture how he liked. He was American and knew all about body language. Like most men from the States, he'd been brought up on psychology.

She ignored the directness of his look and, rolling out the spreadsheet carefully, she bent across the desk and pointed to the bottom. "The name of the architect?"

"Yep? What's up?" He held her gaze with his startling green eyes, which were still pleading for encouragement. However, they were too close together, making Lance look the sharp operator he was.

"Is it Westonman Associates UK?"

"Sure is." He bent forward and squinted at the company details.

"*Shane* Westonman?" He shrugged:

"Dunno. Could be, I guess. The firm was recommended by a guy I know back home. Washington. But, take it from me, whoever he is, I've hired the best in the States. Why?"

"You mean it's an American outfit?" Lorne's heart gave an uncontrolled leap of disappointment. She couldn't believe it wasn't the answer she was hoping for. The name was uncommon. And she was desperate it should be the right 'Westonman Associates'.

But she'd almost given herself away. Lance was staring at her. Calculating. And his tone had been sharp. Suddenly, he was reaching down into the drawer of his desk, pulling out an envelope.

"Here's a letter from the guy." He handed it over. "I've no idea if he's a Yank. Can't you stand another on the project? You're working for one now. Remember."

"Only for the time being," she flashed. "And don't forget it." Lorne didn't need lessons in assertion. She'd learned how to handle men like Lance. They needed standing up to and she could give as good as she got.

Seeing the unmistakable signature at the bottom of the letter sharpened her wits considerably. She'd been right. *It was Shane.* And, in some ways, he was like Lance. Forceful; arrogant often, an excellent business man, but certainly not devious like her present employer. Lance had a super-ego, which didn't always make for perfect staff relations.

"Satisfied?" He was watching her every move. "Keep the letter if you want. Plenty of detail to digest. Now, what's all this about, Lorne?"

"Not much. I'm just curious. I've heard about this firm before and I wondered who was chief executive now." She was sure he didn't believe her, but she certainly wasn't going to tell him any more.

Lance was still staring pointedly when she pushed back her chair and stood up. She was conscious that the taupe silk suit had creased; that the intense heat she felt was from sheer frustration and subdued excitement after looking at that signature. *Shane Westonman*. The man who she'd believed she'd never meet again; whom she'd thought about every day for months.

Lorne folded the spreadsheet carefully and put it, together with the letter, into her light briefcase.

"Come on, honey. I know when something's eating you." Lance had come round the desk swiftly. She swung back her hair, turning away slightly. He was too close. "How do you always manage to look and act so cool?" he added grinning, loosening his tie at the same time. She could smell Cacharel on him. You had to hand it to Lance; he was an extremely sophisticated operator.

She smiled briefly in response, ignoring the question. He would be surprised if he'd known how she really felt. Her whole being was strung-up by just putting the letter with its powerful black-ink signature into the darkness of her briefcase where the contents scored on her heart.

Her head was zinging with memories of the past. She just had to get away from Lance as fast as she could - to think about Shane.

She moved back. "Okay, thanks," she said, "I'll sort out the translations and have them at the builders asap." Suddenly Lance had his hand on her arm. Lorne looked down at the fingers detaining her, wasting every precious second.

"No, *thank you*, Lorne. I'm lucky to have you. And Morton can't wait until tomorrow." Lance was being even slyer, mentioning his seven year old son, who missed his mother dreadfully.

"Can't he?" she answered casually. "I hope he's going to behave on our trip." Like father, like son. Morton was a handful, but she was still fond of the rumbustious, gap-toothed little boy she was taking up the Fire Mountain tomorrow.

8

"He really enjoys being with you, Lorne. Like I do." Lance's eyes were pleading for himself; an open invitation to Lorne to spend their time together. A few months ago, she had found his attentions more welcome, but now she'd learned.

She moved away from him expertly and Lance stood, awkward and seemingly defenceless. It was part of his charm - the little-boy-hurt syndrome. Lorne was almost sorry for him and he would have been even more so for himself, if he'd known the reason she was acting that way. He certainly wouldn't be happy to know about Shane Westonman. He was extremely jealous.

"I'm off now, Lance. Morton will have a great day with the two little girls, I promise. And I have to get this done. I must dash. See you tomorrow."

"Okay." His tone was flat with disappointment. For a moment, Lorne was afraid he was going to try and kiss her, but he only managed to brush against her as she walked towards the door. He didn't try to stop her. He was learning at last that Lorne couldn't be taken for granted. But it had taken a long time to sink in.

* * *

Later, lying on her bed, gave Lorne time to think in privacy. The small bedroom of her flat was cool, its pristine white darkened by closed shutters; Lorne felt quite alone - and glad of it. She put out her hand to her briefcase beside her, and touched it. The soft leather contained Shane's letter, its brief contents crying out to be read just once more.

Feeling inside, she pulled it out again. Her small fingers traced the strong lines of the dashing signature.

It was part of him, enough to make her body tingle with memories and expectation.

She felt *almost* ready to meet him. She was over it now. She wouldn't let him hurt her again. She had loved him so much, but now she was strong enough to hide her feelings. She clutched the letter to her, as if she was holding him. Even the light touch of the paper thrilled her.

The memories were so exciting. And she was bound to see Shane now. He might have broken her heart, but she'd be glad to meet him just one more time.

Suddenly, in her imagination, she was loving him again - whatever he'd done, she still needed him. Slipping the letter under her pillow and marvelling as to why she was being so hopelessly romantic about a man who'd let her down, she closed her eyes, drifting away into dreams of the past. . .

Lorne's head, full of uneasy dreams, tossed about on the pillow and crushed the letter, which curtly informed property magnate, Lance Denver that, in order to discuss the plans for the billion dollar island building project, Shane Westonman would be arriving at Arrecife airport at eleven in the morning the day after tomorrow . . .

* * *

"Gee, is that where the fire lives, Lorne?" Morton's small hand tugged at hers persistently. "Lorne? Is it? Is it, Lorne?" Lance's son, green-eyed too, never gave up.

"What?" Lorne came to, looking down into his face, "Yes, Morton." It wasn't fair to be irritable with him, nor the others. The children couldn't help how she was feeling. She forced herself away from memories of England and Shane, back to what she should be doing, looking after the children.

10

Morton continued to fire questions, pointing excitedly to the gaping hole in the ground from which smoke billowed. One of the mountain wardens approached and Morton and his two small Spanish girl admirers jumped back as, grinning, the swarthy Canarian threw a bucket of water into the hole. It hissed as the mountain's heart angrily spat and sizzled.

"Be careful, Morton," Lorne warned. He was getting very near.

"Is that the volcano?" he shouted, peering down.

"Be careful," she repeated. Morton was too venturesome for his own good. Meanwhile the little girls couldn't contain their excitement, giggling all the time. Lorne was glad the hole wasn't big enough to fall in. Otherwise, all of them would have.

Knowing what imps they were, she allowed the three of them to drag her to the edge. She'd visited the Fire Mountain countless times and the experience was palling. Why had she let Lance talk her into taking Morton and friends? But, after all, he was the boss, and it was holiday time.

Lorne couldn't help smiling. The two girls, Carmen and Michaela were hanging on every word Morton uttered. His brashness towards them reminded her uncomfortably of his father - and she didn't want to think of Lance just then.

"Lorne, can we go to the gift shop now?" demanded her small charge.

"With pleasure," muttered Lorne under her breath, adding aloud, "Yes, if you want. But don't spend *all* your money."

"I got heaps," shouted Morton as he ran off, his baseball cap perched on the back of his head. He chinked the money in his pockets impatiently. "Come on, you two."

"Well, the girls mightn't have," warned Lorne. They

were following Morton hopefully, staring at him with their almost-black eyes.

"Okay, Lorne, I'll give 'em a good time," winked Morton. He was an exhibitionist already. Lorne shook her head at him.

"You're incorrigible, Morton. Go on then. And behave." He returned her a cheeky grin and the next moment the three children were off, their jean-clad legs flashing like blue streaks.

Lorne pulled down her fashionable sunglasses, which had been perched high on her hair and looked round for a place to sit. She could have done without looking after Morton today but, hopefully, he'd find plenty to do in the complex.

She drew the spreadsheet and the architectural plans out of her bag, intending to start on the translation of the technical terms, but her face was burning, and not only from the blazing sun. Rather from her thoughts. She had to admit she liked bringing back those memories which plagued her, however painful.

Although she could hear Morton shouting in the distance, her mind was really thousands of miles away from the barren Canarian landscape. It was sweeping over those glorious, deserted Cornish beaches where she and Shane had walked and made love. . . She came to with a start, feeling the hand on her shoulder, shaking her.

"Hi, Lorne, we're back. Wake up." She opened her eyes. Morton and his girlfriends were regarding her, their grins still apparent behind mountainous ice creams.

"It's all right, I wasn't asleep," Lorne replied. Squinting into the sun, she reached up, and pulled off Morton's cap playfully. Then she put it on her own head. Carmen and Michaela burst into laughter.

Lorne got up. "Right. Come on, you three. Let's go and

12

look at all the things you've missed. Remember, Morton, your dad will want to know all about it when I get you home."

Morton made a face but his moods didn't last as long as his father's; as Lorne folded away the spreadsheet, he'd already got over it and was fooling about with the girls.

Very soon, the long-suffering Lorne was making her way over to the complex with the trio of chattering children jumping about behind her.

* * *

Later, as the coach bumped its way between the black, lava walls and out into the lunar landscape, Lorne was quite relieved the trip was over. She felt exhausted.

Luckily Morton was too tied up with the girls to plague her much. He loved a captive audience; so while he cavorted, Lorne leaned her forehead against the window glass, thinking. Today, she certainly wasn't on top form.

Lance had hired her for the Denver School of English he owned, for several reasons. Primarily, for her qualifications: fluency in Spanish and a teaching certificate. He was no fool. Her degree had pulled off the translation job with his firm as well. She translated project plans and specifications and had become indispensable. Lance couldn't do without her any more. Her looks and personality had scored with the American too. Yet, she had to admit, his interest had been a lifeline when she'd first arrived from England, half out of her mind and her personal life in disarray.

Today, bumping along on the bus from the Fire Mountain, she felt almost as strained as the day she'd arrived on the island. Almost as prickly as the cactus fields, which flashed past the coach windows.

It was no use. Could she bear the chance of having

13

Shane back in her life again? Could she bear it without him? The thought of seeing him again was wonderful; but did she really want even to meet him after all he'd put her through?

She was like her birth sign, Pisces, pulling herself different ways at the same time. She knew the answer to all those questions - in spite of herself. These months away from England had been a respite, but the pain was no better.

Lorne sat, staring at nothing, dredging up Shane's face from the depths of her mind, seeing again those wide, dark eyes; stroking in her imagination the smoothness of his skin, tanned deeply from wintering in exotic places very far from Cornwall; imagining those full, passionate lips and his hard, sweet mouth.

No, the memory of Shane had not dimmed in the slightest, nor what he'd done to her; nor what she'd done to herself. She could remember so many things he said as well.

* * *

Later, with the spreadsheet in front of her once more, Lorne sat on a white chair in the sunniest corner of her flat where the bougainvillaea wound itself round her wrought-iron verandah in cascading flowers, making the cool evening a heaven of colour.

Shane's voice echoed in her ears: "No wonder the kids are crazy about you. I wish I'd had you as a teacher when I was at school." She had kissed the corners of his teasing lips and he'd taught her things about loving she'd never known existed in spite of her air of sophistication and her travelling abroad.

"You could have been anything with those brains and looks. You're beautiful. But you're here. In my village."

14

And he'd stroked her cheek tenderly. He could talk. Shane looked more like a Hollywood heart-throb than a London-based architect, commuting at weekends to see his mother in Cornwall.

To think it had all gone wrong. That she had messed up her life. Lorne stared at the delicate fan spread out on her wall and the tears came into her eyes.

"Why did you make me fall in love with you, Shane?" she said out loud. And there was only the lizard who lived in the stone wall to hear the break in her voice. Since meeting Shane, she hadn't been the same. At twenty-one, she'd believed in love at first sight. Now Lorne was wiser, or thought she was, until Lance had handed her *his* letter, signed in black ink.

Lorne just had to face it. It was still Shane and Cornwall - twined round her heart like the wild flowers in the deep Cornish lanes. And here she was on an island in the middle of the Atlantic. She had run away, taken the only way out she could. But she was unable to lie to herself any more. Whatever had happened, and she still couldn't understand why, it was there constantly. That old flame, burning with white-hot intensity. She loved Shane and he had been in love with someone else. It was quite simple. The thought of Moyra Trevise and her last meeting with her rival made Lorne feel quite miserably sick. . .

* * *

She forced herself to finish the translation for the builders. There were a few unfamiliar technical terms, but she had a good dictionary. Translating for Lance paid too well to be ignored. She was still staring at the monitor of her computer when the door bell rang.

It was Lance. He kissed her 'Hello' in the Spanish way on both cheeks, like friends do. But he wanted to be more than friends. Lorne regarded the well-built older man as he pulled up a chair near to the screen, beside hers.

They had a strange relationship. Once, he'd been her saviour, but they'd never been lovers. She had held off. Lorne knew she'd hurt Lance; realised how much he wanted their relationship to develop; that he was still hoping; that he didn't understand her attitude. But it had been the same with every man since Shane.

Suddenly Lorne was asking herself if she could ever love anyone else. There was plenty of time. Her therapist had told her what she felt was quite common after such an experience. "Give it time," he'd said. He was so different from the abrupt hospital consultant she'd seen in England - approachable, sympathetic, relaxed. And she believed him. She swallowed as she looked at the screen - and Lance had caught the vibes.

"Is it that difficult?" he asked, looking at the display.

"A bit," she confessed. "I've had to look up a few things for the specifications." She was relieved he wasn't pressing her like he'd done the day before. They continued making small talk.

"Morton had a great time. He can't stop talking about the devil in the volcano. Too much television, of course. He didn't even stop when Granma put him to bed. But he soon towed the line. One thing my mother knows is how to handle kids. Like always." Lilly Denver handled her grandson like she'd done her son.

After Lance's wife had run off with one of his partners she'd stepped in and made a new life for both of them. Lilly was one hell of a lady.

"Of course she's always telling me that what Morton needs is a mother." Then Lorne could see what was coming next. So she deflected the conversation skilfully.

"These plans are great, Lance." She knew he couldn't

16

resist flattery. And talking about Shane must do her good. "And Westonman is coming himself to go over them?"

"Sure. I'm surprised though. It's a big firm and the boss doesn't just come running to a little island like this, however swell a contract. I guess it means he's impressed with us too."

"I can't wait to meet him," replied Lorne, her heart fluttering.

"You can't. You seem real interested in this guy."

Her stomach lurched. "No, it's not that. I'm just excited about getting the best for your project. For the firm - and the island of course." It was a neat white lie, with some element of truth.

"You said you'd heard of the firm before? And Shane Westonman?"

"It may be a different man. Mine was English. The firm I mean. Possibly related." That threw Lance off the scent; he spent the next ten minutes talking about the plans and nothing else. She didn't return to the subject of the architect again because she knew he'd be even more suspicious.

Lance lingered over the glass of wine she offered him. Afterwards, over his coffee. Lorne couldn't just ask him to leave, but she wanted to be alone with her thoughts. And he must have sensed it.

"Well, I guess I shouldn't hold you up any longer." He put down his cup. Outside, the crickets seemed to be making more noise than usual, filling the humid night with infuriating energy. Their sound made her nerves jangle.

Lance's green eyes held questions still. She could see he was hoping this time she'd let him kiss her properly, but she gave him no encouragement. Instead he bent and kissed her on the cheek. "I know a brush-off when I see it," he joked. "You look all-in, Lorne. I suggest you leave

17

the rest of the translation for a couple of days. There's plenty of time.

"Oh, by the way, there is something else that I'd like you to do for me. And you'll be able to ask Westonman all those questions yourself. You're scheduled to meet him at the airport. Instead of me.

"Don't look like that. He can't be that boring. You won't have to drive. I'll send you in the limo." Her face must have been as pale as she felt.

Lance's limo was well known on the island. He'd had it imported. In Lanzarote where people drove small cars, her American boss's was the biggest. He employed a chauffeur too.

"I'm meeting him?" she repeated, hoping her voice didn't sound too shaky. "Why?"

"Because I'm playing golf, honey, and I can't get out of it. And also you're the only one on my team who speaks perfect English. It should impress him." He grinned.

"But I've the shopping and . . ." Now it had come to it, she was afraid to meet Shane. She couldn't bear it.

"Sorry, honey. I've promised Miguel two rounds. And he *is* putting in half the cash. You don't mind, do you? I suppose I could ask. . ."

"No, it's okay. I'll go." No way could she let anyone else meet Shane. She realised she was behaving quite irrationally, but that was the effect the letter had had on her.

"Okay. Fine." Lance looked relieved, but puzzled. "He's booked in at the Rio Grande. You could take him straight there. And tell him I'll meet you both at twelve-thirty for lunch. Okay?"

"Great." How she sounded so calm she couldn't imagine.

"Take care then." Lance hesitated, still hoping she would kiss him. Instead, she opened the door and smiled.

18

"Have a nice day," she said. He acknowledged the slight sarcasm with good-humoured acceptance. When Lance left, Lorne was numb with shock, but alive with anticipation. How was she going to get through until eleven? And when she got to the airport, what on earth would she and Shane Westonman say to each other after not seeing each other for so long?

* * *

CHAPTER 2

It was only a small plane and had come from London. Lorne wondered why Shane had stopped over from Washington. Or had he just switched flights?

It was even hotter that day; there was sand in the air, which meant most Canarians would stay inside until the cooler evening. Even though Lorne was used to the heat, it was punishing. If it hadn't been for the constant breeze it would have been unbearable. She was very glad of the limousine's air conditioning, which was very different from travelling in her own small Seat.

The road to Arrecife had seemed never-ending. As Lance's chauffeur drove on through clouds of swirling dust, Lorne leaned back, watching the heavy passing traffic and the planes coming in low, wondering if Shane was on one of them. It wouldn't be long now until she knew.

Later, she wandered up and down the Arrivals area, which was small in comparison with a lot of airports. She stared through the dark, plate glass, shielded by a profusion of exotic green plants, thinking all the time about the man she was there to meet. Was he living in Washington permanently now? Had he left the London firm and set up another company of his own? But she couldn't imagine him leaving England for good.

Lorne was becoming more nervous as she waited. Was he still with Moyra? He might even be married to her.

Anything could have happened if what Moyra had said was true. It was the last thought that made Lorne feel particularly miserable. Sick and jealous all at once. She was behaving like a fool, but it was her heart's fault. Her head wanted her to be otherwise; never to be hurt again.

Perhaps she ought to have taken Lance up on his offer of a relationship? He was what her mother would have called *a good catch*. Wealthy, available and he cared about her. In fact, he would do anything for her. If she gave Lance the slightest encouragement that way, he'd propose.

Lorne stood, weighing the pros and cons in her mind. She also liked it here in the Canary Islands. She had a good job, her colleagues were mainly ex-pats and most weren't looking for promotion. The way was wide open for Lorne to make a success of her professional and personal life. Even the irrepressible Morton was fond of her.

Lorne knew she ought to forget Shane, should have done so long ago. If she had, she wouldn't have been feeling like this. But, deep within, a little voice kept reminding her she could never marry Lance Denver. Even if she stayed single all her life.

How can you do this to yourself, you fool? she scolded under her breath. *Are you going to let him ruin your life again and tear yourself in pieces when you see him?*

Lorne sat down, her legs weak, her head in her hands. *Damn you, Shane, for coming back into my life and turning it upside down,* she muttered, re-living the past. How could she have guessed what would happen when she first met Shane Westonman? But there had been signs. . .

* * *

Lorne hadn't felt responsible enough teaching Sixth Form

Spanish to girls only three years her junior. At twenty-one it hadn't been an option she considered after three years' study and one year's back-packing in Spain. She would have liked to have kept on drifting but, after several adventures, there still seemed nothing special in her life. It had been a lot of laughs, but now she needed a career.

Her father had seen the advertisement first. He'd held out the *Times Educational Supplement* and pointed:

"How about this one, Lorne? Seaview Independent School for Girls. And it's for teaching Spanish. As for the place - well - perfect, I'd say. Westonman. Cornwall. I used to be stationed down there in the RAF. But that was before I met your mother." He grinned. "Scenery's wonderful. People take some getting used to strangers though. But I'd go for it, Lorne."

At that time she'd thought it was luck. Much later she knew it had been Fate. She'd been given the post *and* Shane in the first term. She remembered their meeting so well.

She'd been standing waiting for the school minibus outside the lych gate of Westonman Church where she'd taken a First Year class to a Christmas carol practice. While she and a few of the girls were looking at how many berries there were on the holly hedge and chattering about the holiday, ten year old Sally Curtis, another mischief like Morton Denver, had been fooling about at the back of the line.

The next moment, and if Lorne hadn't screamed out, the little girl would have been crushed under the wheels of a Land Rover which had come far too fast round the corner. Lorne had hugged the terrified child to her as the tall man in waxed jacket and wellingtons jumped down from the vehicle.

"What the hell was that child doing?" he shouted.

Lorne glared at him. "It was just as much your fault. You were going too fast. We didn't expect anyone to come round the bend like that."

"I could see that." The man was unbelievably arrogant. His eyes, like sparky fire, glinted in a deep tanned face, which showed he was used to wintering in more exotic places than Westonman. In fact, his skin colour almost matched his deep brown hair, streaked with hazel lights.

Lorne, badly-shaken by the incident, felt tense and annoyed by his high-handed attitude. She wasn't going to be spoken to like that in front of her pupils. Besides, it wasn't her fault. But, evidently, he hadn't finished what he intended to say.

"So you're the new teacher. I'd have thought they would have taught you some road sense in London." Lorne's eyes were glinting too by now. She tossed her fair hair back over the hood of her duffel coat.

"Yes, and in London you'd have hit someone driving like that." It was a silly remark, but it made an impression. The man was frowning. "You could have killed Sally," reproved Lorne.

"I could have - but I didn't."

The next moment the man was stooping to see if Sally was hurt anywhere. His eyes, which had been so challenging a moment before, were full of anxiety as he looked up at Lorne. "She seems okay."

Lorne had never seen anyone change mood so quickly. A moment ago he'd been ready for a fight, now he looked sorry and relieved all at once. He brushed the little girl's navy anorak down.

"There. You're okay. And don't ever do that again, Sally. Or you might be spending Christmas in hospital. Understand?" Sally, near to tears and biting her lip, nodded. "My regards to your mother." Lorne was amazed. He must know Sally's family.

Then he turned to her again. "And, whatever you're thinking, I do realise looking after so many kids at once isn't easy. I don't envy you. But - you need eyes in the back of your head. Good afternoon." He'd managed to have the last word after all. Then he was pulling himself up into the Land Rover.

With a curt nod, he switched on the ignition and, with the slightest of acknowledgements, accelerated away. Later, Lorne realised that was the nearest Shane Westonman ever got to saying sorry.

Safe in the minibus with a chastened Sally beside her, Lorne asked, "Did you know that man, Sally?"

She nodded. "Yes, Miss Blair. It was Mr Westonman - from the Manor. I live just down the road."

So - it was the son and heir. And he was one of Seaview's governors. The reason they'd never met before was because he'd been abroad when she was interviewed.

Lorne breathed a sigh of relief at the thought. She'd heard a few stories about him already - and they weren't all roses. *Extremely attractive. Ridiculously arrogant.* That's what Jane had called him and she knew about everyone as the local doctor's wife. Lorne had a flat in her lovely Georgian home. Jane used to be the practice nurse until she married Dr John Steele and now she was a part-time matron at Seaview.

Lorne remembered thinking no wonder Shane Westonman was still single, as the minibus made its way back to the school, skirting the low stone wall which bordered his estate. No woman would put up with such high-handed behaviour. He needed taking in hand.

The morning after the incident also stuck fast in her memory. A white van arrived outside the doctor's house while Lorne was putting up her new curtains. She watched the driver go round to the back of the van, open the doors and withdraw a large bouquet swathed in cellophane.

She was amazed to hear the doorbell to her flat. Running downstairs quickly, a surprised Lorne received the flowers. With trembling fingers she undid the red, silk bow, taking off the wrapping to reveal twenty beautiful red roses. The message on the card read simply:

> *I'll look out for you next time.*
> *Shane Westonman.*

When Jane saw the flowers, her eyebrows lifted in surprise. "You've met Shane then? You must have made a hit."

"No, he was the one who nearly did that. He could have killed Sally with his driving. I thought he was very rude. In fact I could have killed *him*. But, next minute he changed entirely."

"That's Shane all over." Jane smiled. "But deep down he's all right. He must be to come and see his mother so often. She's not that easy to get on with. His heart's in the right place. He loves this area and, although he's away most of the time, he always comes back. You know he has projects all over the world. His company's one of the best."

"And he comes home to see his mother often?" Lorne looked at the flowers, wondering when she'd see him again.

"Amongst others."

"Others?" asked Lorne.

"Well," added Jane, "Moyra Trevise for one. They say he'll marry her eventually."

"Who's she?" asked Lorne lightly, staring at the flowers.

"Oh, she used to go to Seaview. Then they sent her to

25

another boarding school in the South East. She and Shane have known each other for yonks."

"Have I ever met her?" Suddenly it was most important to know.

"If you had, you wouldn't have forgotten," replied Jane pointedly. "I wonder what she'd say if she saw these? Watch out, Lorne."

"What do you mean?"

"What I said. Watch out. People can be very funny round here. And Moyra's family is still local. She comes back too, like Shane." It was then that Lorne had remembered her father's warning when he'd first seen the advert for the job. And that had been the beginning of it all . . .

* * *

Lorne sighed as she remembered. She got up and went over to see if the plane's passengers had embarked yet, her heart thudding uncomfortably. She hoped they wouldn't take too long. Lance's limo was taking a lot of space right outside the doors and the airport police were hot on parking.

Lorne looked across the tarmac at the plane. She gasped. The hot wind full of stinging Sahara sand was whipping the dark hair away from the forehead of the man, pausing in the doorway.

Lorne saw the unmistakable line of Shane's square shoulders under the fashionable light-coloured suit jacket and the familiar athletic stance. *He hadn't changed.* In those few short seconds, she was remembering every lovely moment between them.

The strangest feelings ran through her body as Lorne watched Shane disembarking. It was as if months hadn't passed at all. How could she still love him so much? Then he was suddenly standing back to let someone through first.

26

The woman was tall but slight, her fashionable short skirt revealing elegant legs. The wind tossed her hair back from her face. It needn't have. She was instantly recognisable. Moyra Trevise.

Then quickly the couple were coming down the steps. And Shane overtook Moyra and waited to help her . . . Lorne felt frozen with cold on that hot morning. Her moment of sheer, mad excitement had suddenly changed to miserable disappointment. Moyra and Shane. *No, nothing had changed.* They were together. And she was supposed to meet them. Talk to them. She couldn't. She just couldn't. She knew she was going to chicken out.

Lorne hurried across the Arrivals area - towards the door, conscious of prickling tears behind her eyes. She must find a way out . . .

Juan, Lance's driver nodded: "*Si, si, senorita,* I understand. Senor Westonman. I take him and the lady straight to the Rio Grande, check them in and let Senor Lance know?"

"Yes, you go in and meet them now. You can't miss them. They'll be coming through any minute. And - if Senor Denver wants to know what happened, tell him I wasn't feeling well and I've gone home in a cab. Tell him - it was unavoidable." Juan looked worried.

"You sure you're all right, *senorita?*"

"It's just the heat, Juan," she lied. "I felt faint in there. And they're very important clients. Senor Denver wouldn't want anything to go wrong. I'd rather be at my best when we meet. Now go, please."

Lorne was so thankful she hadn't brought her own car. Later, as the cab swung through the parking lanes, Lorne put up a hand to wipe away a tear. She hardly ever cried. She'd done enough of that in the past.

She tried to pull herself together. And how was she

27

going to keep out of Shane and Moyra's way while they were on the island? It was going to be impossible. She couldn't make up being ill for a week.

Her stomach churned miserably. And there was no way she could tell Lance about her and Shane. . .

* * *

Some time later, Lorne let Lance into the flat. She'd been expecting the visit.

"What made you take off like that? I got some rigmarole from Juan about you and the heat." Lance's green eyes narrowed. He was evidently not feeling sympathetic. But breaking into Lance's golf was a very serious matter.

"I was feeling ill."

"You look fine now." His eyes raked over her. Lorne was suddenly annoyed. She was very much on edge and she didn't need this attitude from him.

Also, by late afternoon, she'd convinced herself it was the heat that had prompted her impulsive behaviour; that she didn't care about Shane and Moyra; that it was only the shock of seeing they were still together which had made her feel ill. And she *had* been sick.

"I don't feel it," she retorted in answer. She was also in no mood for Lance's compliments. Whenever he told her she looked fine, he meant something else. He was extraordinarily selfish. Of course the underlying reason for his behaviour was the interruption of his game.

His next movement really took her by surprise. He had his arms round her.

"What are you doing? Let me go."

"Not before you tell me what's really the matter. You know you're lovely." She pushed away from him.

"Let go." The violence of her tone must have surprised him. He did quickly, putting up his arms in a gesture of surrender.

"Okay. Have it your way. But you're one hell of a tease." She could stomach his ego, but not his insensitivity.

"Leave me alone, Lance," she flashed. "No one asked you to come here." She felt shaky, not because of his unwelcome attentions, but from relief he'd taken notice. She put some distance between them. "I want you to go. Please."

"You've made that damn clear. But I need you tonight."

"What?"

"*Work*, honey. Business. I want you with me. We're having dinner with Westonman. And his girl friend." Lance winked. "I didn't know he was bringing her along."

As Lance went on and on about Moyra, just one name was flying round in Lorne's head driving out every other sensible thought. *Shane*. How could she sit opposite him and Moyra at dinner, pretending she didn't care. Her legs felt weak. She sat down suddenly. Lance was staring.

"Hey, you're really not well. Hang on, I'll fetch you some water." Then he rushed off to the kitchen while Lorne sat, her mind totally blanked out. Next moment he was handing her a glass. "It's okay if you can't make it."

"No, I can," replied Lorne, coming to. She had to get over this once and for all. She would stop behaving like some wimpish Victorian heroine and face him. "It's just the heat I can't handle today," she heard herself saying.

It was only when Lance had gone that Lorne was remembering the last awful words Moyra Trevise had taunted her with. *You don't count. Shane and I were made for each other. If only you hadn't come on the scene, everything would have been all right* . . . That was when Lorne had finally decided to get out. Of his life. Away from England. From all the memories. And now, it looked as though what Moyra had said was true. She and Shane were together. And he'd forgotten Lorne.

* * *

"Hello." Shane's voice was deep and husky as ever. Any nearer and she could have touched his body. He listened attentively to Lance's introduction just as if he'd never met her before.

"Lorne, Shane Westonman. Shane, Lorne Blair, my assistant on the project."

"Mr Westonman," she said, extending her hand, trembling with the thought of his touch. Her voice seemed very far away.

"Miss Blair." Then his hand was in hers, burning her palm with the touch she'd longed for; her fingers imprisoned in the warm grip. And he was on his own. No Moyra with him.

Lorne's heart beat so fast she could hardly breathe. The power he exuded had not dimmed one bit since she'd lost him. And she had to keep pretending, like him. But when he'd turned from the bar, when she and Lance had first walked in, he'd almost given himself away. Especially when his eyes had held her deep-sapphire glance.

But next moment he'd recovered that self-control she'd seen so many times. He had pulled himself together as well as she had, but Lorne had felt one tiny triumphant moment that her presence had knocked him off-balance.

Now his dark eyes were probing hers and the hint of a smile on his lips mocked her. "In what capacity do you assist Lance, Miss Blair?" He knew how to rouse her emotions. But his mockery was teasing, rather than cruel.

She accepted the challenge. "I'll fill you in later." If she'd been over-sensitive, she could have taken the remark as an insult.

Then Lance cut in: "In every way. I couldn't do without her." He was squeezing her arm. Lorne froze. Shane's expressive eyebrows rose quizzically.

"Evidently." Then changing the subject, he added dismissively. "I've ordered champagne."

"Great," grinned Lance. Lorne watched silently as the white-jacketed waiter filled the three flutes with the delicate, effervescent, pink liquid.

The zest rose and burst against her lips as she sipped from the glass Shane handed to her, allowing his fingers to brush against hers slightly, making her as dizzy with his touch as if she'd drunk ten glasses of Moet-Chandon. Then he was lifting his glass. She and Lance followed suit.

"To the success of the project." They drank the toast. She looked up, knowing she was going to have to say it, however personal it sounded.

"Lance tells me you aren't here alone?" Lance was glancing at her. Her own words set her teeth on edge, like the squeak of a board-rubber. "Are you making a holiday of the trip?" *She just had to know about Moyra and their relationship.*

He looked down at her. She couldn't imagine what he was thinking. His jaw was set, tanned skin stretched tightly over his strong cheekbones. It was a handsome mask of a face. He leaned slightly against the bar. There was only one inch separating them now, one more and she could have felt his heart beating under the dinner jacket.

"She's resting," he said. "And, no, this won't be anything like a vacation." The slight Americanism startled Lorne.

31

"So Miss Trevise won't be joining us?" asked Lance regretfully.

"Not at the moment," replied Shane. He had his eyes on Lorne, who was suddenly extremely conscious that her off-the-shoulder black cocktail dress revealed the top of her cleavage. She couldn't read anything in his eyes, except admiration.

"Jet lag?" persisted Lance, making Lorne quite angry inside. His ebullient stupidity was heightened by Shane's wonderful *savoir-faire*.

"Kind of." American accent again. It must have rubbed off in Washington. "We're on a heavy schedule. She decided to take a rain-check but she'll be back to normal tomorrow."

"What a pity," said Lorne. Shane's eyes narrowed and she saw secret amusement that made her heart leap for joy. Perhaps he didn't care about Moyra's jet-lag? "I'd have loved to have met her," she finished triumphantly.

"She might join us later," replied Shane, and the twinkle of amusement vanished for Lorne, who took a quick sip of champagne. *How dare you tease me?* she asked mentally, the spell broken.

"Great!" said Lance. "In any case you'd have met her tomorrow, honey. I have the whole thing fixed. Do you play golf, Shane?" Lorne had one dreadful moment thinking of having to entertain Moyra while the men went off, but Shane saved her.

"No. I prefer more strenuous sports." She breathed again but she couldn't have imagined how wonderful and how awful this dinner date with Shane was proving to be.. How was she going to get through the whole evening?

* * *

CHAPTER 3

Shane sat down opposite her. Lorne's heart skipped; even the palms of her hands were tingling. She felt sensitive, alive, as if an electric current was coursing through every vein in her body.

Shane had lost none of his good looks but, somehow, somewhere, Lorne could sense a difference. He couldn't be called jaded or cynical, it was just that his worldly experience seemed to be showing. Perhaps some of the youthful zest had gone? Maybe Shane had moved on, like she had. Grown-up?

With a pang, she noted the dark wings of hair above his ears were tinged with tiniest tips of grey. He was too young to be grey. What had he been through? *Then she told herself off for caring.* Here she was, making allowances for *him. What had she been through?* Just being here tonight and facing him had been awful.

He settled himself at the table, his tan even more striking against the stark white of his ruffled evening shirt. A ridiculous stab of pride went through her. He was the handsomest man in the room. Then she reminded herself that he wasn't hers any more. That he belonged to someone else. That their love affair was over. Yet his liquid-dark eyes, half-veiled by the lashes almost too long and too luxurious for a man, were sending those old familiar messages which assaulted her senses like the wine which was now being poured.

"Darling, you look wonderful tonight." Lorne came to. *Lance had his hand over hers.* What was he playing at? But suddenly and irrationally, she wanted Shane to know that the last months hadn't been wasted mooning over him. Then, immediately, like the Piscean she was, she was afraid Shane mightn't show any more interest.

"Are you sure you're feeling okay, honey?" added Lance. Shane's narrowed eyes watched the by-play.

"Perfectly, thank you." She withdrew her hand. Lance was turning to Shane.

"Lorne's been off colour since this morning. The heat."

"Is that right?" Shane's eyes searched her face. It was then she wondered how he and Moyra really got on. Two strong wills, his unbending; hers, petulant and spoiled. But Lorne supposed given what they shared, they'd make a go of it.

"Sure is," replied Lance. "She couldn't make it to meet you. Had to leave at the airport." Lorne could have killed Lance.

"You mean this morning?" asked Shane.

"Spot on. She was scheduled to meet you and Moyra. The welcoming party. But she had to go home in a cab."

"I'm sorry," said Shane, looking her full in the eyes. That simple little apology was the first he'd ever offered. Was it meant to cover all their lost time together? Lorne knew he realised she'd chickened out of meeting them at the airport.

If they'd been alone, she would have let fly at him, battered him with her fists, yelled out all that pent-up emotion, hurt him as he'd hurt her, but all she could do was sit like a lemon saying nothing. She felt extremely hot. To cover her angry confusion, she adjusted her napkin.

34

But when she looked up, his eyes were raking her face as if he'd never seen her before. Strangely. Hungrily. *And he had no right*. She calmed herself as the waiter handed round the menus, using hers to hide her face in case it gave away how she was feeling. The men's voices seemed to be coming from the distance.

"I suggest the salmon mousse. The seafood's excellent here . . ." That was Lance.

"Followed by the sea-food platter . . ." Shane.

"Yep, Canarian speciality. I love sea-food. Always have it back home. Cape Cod . . ." Lorne lowered the menu. She had to speak some time. She might as well keep up the pretence.

"Are you American, Shane?" His eyes held hers.

"No. English. Cornish, rather. Do you know Cornwall?" She breathed in. *How she knew Cornwall*. His eyes were urging her on. To tell him how much she knew it.

"I was there once." How was he feeling now? Like her? Could he hear all those silent *whys* pouring out of her heart. Her whole being was one mix of their emotion . . .

And things didn't improve. Lorne's mind could concentrate on nothing but Shane. When he and Lance talked business, she found she wasn't listening, even though she should have been. It was desperation wanting something you knew was bad for you, but when you got it, it was both wicked and wonderful.

As Shane's powerful throat coped expertly with the local oysters, she was remembering someone had told her they were aphrodisiacs. And the evening slipped on and on . . .

* * *

The small dance floor was made of heavy glass with lighting hidden beneath. Couples were dancing intimately, swaying over it and Lorne was willing him to ask her. But Shane's face showed he was weighing up the relationship between her and Lance.

Shane watched them dancing and every time they passed him by, he was leaning back in his chair, his dark eyes following her every move like a hunter, fixing on his prey.

Lorne just wanted the evening to be over. Or to be in Shane's arms. To feel his body against hers; snuggle into that familiar scent which brought the memories tumbling back with aching sweetness.

She wanted to forget the past; to enjoy just one more of those wonderful moments they'd shared. She and Lance walked off the dance floor with Lorne expertly slipping her arm out of her boss's.

"My turn?" said Shane. The moment had come. "That's if you'd like to?" The answer came easily but the excitement left her breathless. She looked at him, fascinated by that mobile and expressive mouth, working into a smile. She imagined kissing and kissing his lips.

"I'd like," she answered. His hand was resting on her waist as he began to lead her on to the floor. It was heaven - then hell. Their way was blocked by a svelte figure sheathed in silk, voluptuous breasts thrusting from her low-cut gown.

"Moyra." Shane's voice was measured and controlled. Had he felt Lorne tremble? There was hostile amazement on Moyra's beautifully made-up face.

"You?" Her eyebrows were arched.

"Me." Lorne breathed in. Suddenly she could feel Shane's hand on her elbow. She looked into his face. He was staring hard at Moyra.

"Back to the table." It was a command. She turned mechanically with Moyra on his other side. Naturally he didn't want a scene. And Moyra went for the jugular. Lance was standing up, admiring eyes on Moyra. Suddenly Lorne could see how tightly Shane was holding her elbow.

"Moyra. Lance Denver. Lance, Moyra." Lorne's heart was plummeting as Moyra shook hands with Lance. Her dream was turning into a nightmare. Then Shane added, his voice level and calm, "And - you've met Lorne already. She's Lance's assistant." But there was an edge to the last sentence which Lorne recognised. He was warning Moyra to keep her mouth shut.

Moyra laughed. Then, flicking a glance in Lorne's direction which said, *Okay, I'll play along with this farce,* she held out two hands to Shane:

"Isn't that the lambada, darling? I'd love to do it with you." Lorne's heart was battering in her ears. She watched dully as Moyra slipped her hands underneath Shane's arms, making a quick, fluid movement.

Lorne's eyes took in those beautiful, little hands, the great diamond ring on the third finger of her left sparkling, caressing Shane, cajoling him then, next moment, Moyra was pulling him on to the dance floor.

Lorne swallowed as Lance finally took his eyes off Moyra's svelte figure and turned to her, "Lucky swine. What about it then, Lorne? Shall we lambada as well?"

"No, thank you. I'll sit this one out," she said.

Lance shrugged: "Okay. Another drink?"

She shook her head miserably. All she could see was the deliberate, seductive way Moyra moved sinuously in Shane's arms, her slim hands about his neck; the dress, slashed to the thigh, exposing her legs. . .

Lorne felt sick. She couldn't take it any more. The sophisticated, carefree image she'd tried so hard to create since she lost Shane, was crumbling. And the old Lorne was back, laid bare, cut to the heart.

"Magnificent." Lorne heard Lance speak through a surprisingly sudden haze of tears. She realised the admiring remark was reserved for Moyra. "What a couple," he added jealously, watching their every move.

Lorne's head was bent over her handbag. She didn't want him to see she was upset. If only he knew what Moyra was really like. Men could be such fools.

"What are you doing, honey?" Lorne was gathering her things.

"I'm going home," Lorne said. "I'm not feeling well again." She was so thankful she had an excuse to get away.

"Home?" His expression was blank. "But you can't. Not now. I need you."

"I'm sorry," she said, "but I'll be no use to you like this, Lance." He was getting on his feet. "No, don't bother. I'll find a cab. No, honestly, I don't want you to take me. I'll be okay on my own. Think of the business."

He was staring at her uncertainly.

"Please, Lance," she added, "you enjoy the rest of the evening. I haven't been feeling well since I left the airport." At least that was true. "Perhaps the oysters didn't agree with me?"

He nodded.

She put a hand over her mouth - to stop herself from crying.

"You poor kid, you're really sick." He waved to a waiter, who rushed over. "Call a cab."

The man hurried off. The lambada was finishing and Lorne couldn't stand one more minute of seeing Moyra and Shane. She got up.

Suddenly, Shane was striding towards her with Moyra flouncing behind him. His quick eyes were taking in the situation. "Lorne?"

38

"The heat - and, maybe, the oysters. I called a cab," said Lance. Lorne couldn't trust herself to look Shane in the eyes. Nor could she stand the sight of Moyra.

"You poor thing. Just as we were all beginning to enjoy ourselves." Moyra's false words echoed in her ears.

"I'm sorry. Excuse me, please." Lorne reached for her wrap. Suddenly, she felt Shane's strong hands arranging it round her shoulders. She shivered violently at his touch.

"I'll see to the cab," he said to Lance as the waiter came over. His commanding tone brooked no refusal. "You look after Moyra, Lance. She deserves a good time."

"Sure thing," replied Lance with alacrity. Then Shane was guiding Lorne through the tables towards the foyer. He didn't speak but her whole body was conscious of his protecting arm.

They reached the door. As the night air blew into her face, Lorne breathed in deeply. She couldn't go on like this. It was no use. The cool wind was beginning to revive her and she was angry with herself for showing her feelings.

She'd survived without him for so long she hadn't realised how painful it would really be seeing Shane again. But she had to go on surviving. It had to be all over between them. Just had to be. She couldn't stand Shane not being hers.

They stood in silence as the cab driver came round and opened the door. Shane was still holding on to her arm. What *could* they say to each other after what had happened between them. The whole thing was terrible.

There were so many things she wanted to say to him. To tell him. "Thank you, Shane. I'll be all right now," she said. It was all she could manage.

She lifted her eyes and saw, with a shock, there was agony in his. "Please, Shane, I have to go. Please, let me go," she added. He withdrew his hand. In a moment, she was inside and, as the driver slammed the door to, she couldn't bear to look into his eyes again.

As the car accelerated, her last glimpse of Shane was blurred by angry, uncontrollable tears. . .

* * *

Lorne woke with a start at three in the morning. For a minute she couldn't think what dreadful thing had happened and then the memory of the whole awful evening came rushing back.

Her eyes felt uncomfortable and swollen from crying in her sleep. From mourning those lovely, lost, precious moments they'd spent together. Her head was aching as she stared into the dark, which seemed to close round her. She buried her face in the pillow and tried to tell herself she'd feel better in the daylight, but she knew she was lying. Would she ever get over Shane Westonman?

Lorne drifted back into her dreams of the past. If only she had been able to tell Shane all she'd been through after the break-up. But she couldn't have risked it. Couldn't have kept him that way. Couldn't have let him know the agony of the painful secret, which she had ended up facing alone.

Lorne tossed to and fro as she thought of what had happened after they split. Then she remembered the look in his eyes as she got into the cab. What was she going to do? Did he want her again? She wanted him. But he had Moyra Trevise now. And maybe everything he needed.

The battering of her heart seemed to fill the bedroom, thumping hard in her ears, sickening her - and then she realised someone was knocking on her door. *At this time. Who could it be? What had happened?*

Suddenly, Lorne was out of her sleep and into reality.

She reached for her robe and threw it on. A moment later, she was switching on the light and hurrying out of the bedroom, feeling the cold marble tiles under her bare feet as she crossed through the dimness of her living area, broken only by the shaft of warm light from her room.

She pushed her hair out of her eyes. Three in the morning. *Be careful, Lorne*, she said to herself. Suddenly the knocking stopped. Whoever it was had heard her coming.

Lorne stood uncertainly. Then, making sure the chain was on, she opened the door a crack.

"Who is it?"

"Me."

"You!" gasped Lorne. She opened the chain fully. Shane was still in his dinner jacket. One stupid thought suddenly came into her head. What a mess she must look. "What do you want?"

"To talk to you." His voice was husky and his eyes very bright.

"There's no point," she said, her voice shaking. She forced a sob back.

"Please let me in, Lorne." Next moment, she was sliding the chain off. "There's always a point," he said, as he stepped inside the hall and looked down at her. She swallowed. "You're shaking," he said softly. "Are you cold?"

She wasn't. Just that the knocking had scared her - and that he was so near. Suddenly, he took her hands in his and began to chafe them wordlessly. And he was looking into her eyes. She caught her breath and was trying to pull herself together.

"Where's Moyra?" She just had to say it.

"Where she belongs." What did he mean? Lorne was

quite breathless. Suddenly, Shane bent his head to her, breathed in and caught her in his arms. She felt him bring her up against his warm, strong body.

"Please, Shane, please," she breathed weakly. But she knew she wasn't begging him to stop.

"I want you, Lorne. God, how I want you."

She was dizzy as he said the words she'd wanted to hear all through those last, long months. There was no reason in her head then, just a mad desire to hear his voice and be his again. As they stood in the dark hall, the whole of her body thrilled to his caresses; tiny intimate kisses as he nuzzled the base of her neck, making sweet, little movements, driving away regrets and reproaches.

She responded in the same way, kissing his neck and jaw line. She felt him murmur in pleasure and, in a moment, they were swept away in the strongest rush of passion either had ever felt. All she was conscious of in those wonderful seconds, were his sighs of excitement as he discovered she was naked under her robe.

Months of pain fell away as quickly as the soft terry towelling. Then she was naked against him; his half-closed eyes raking over her face and her body hungrily. Holding her close and both shivering with delight and anticipation, she was helping him take off his ruffled shirt and tie. . .

She moaned with pleasure as her hands roved over his smooth skin. Her breasts tingled as she touched him; inside, deep throbs of desire racked her. Her feelings were stronger than she could have ever imagined. She murmured words she didn't want him to hear, "No, Shane, we shouldn't, please, please . . ."

"We should, we should, come on. . ." Somewhere, in the distance, her brain was telling her there was no sense in this - but her body and her soul wanted all of him. Now!

"Oh, Shane . . ." His kiss was deep as his body pressed against hers. Half of her was alive to the kiss; half, to the knowledge that his hands were loosening the satin cummerbund of his evening trousers . . .

The tightening between her legs showed her muscles knew better from sheer, beautiful instinct as the front of Shane's naked thighs pressed against hers, soft and yielding. His tongue searched her mouth frantically and she opened it wide beneath his lips and its hard curl was inside, filling hers with delight.

Shane's hands were round her waist now, pressing into the small of her back, stroking and kneading. In sheer abandonment, her own hands slipped round his waist, down above his narrow hips, down again to the tight hollow which finished in his neat, rounded buttocks. Lorne grasped them and he shivered and moaned in delight.

Next moment, she was in his arms and he was carrying her out of the darkness of the hall, across the dim living space into the warmth and light of her bedroom. . .

As Shane put her down, they stood close together naked and her hands slipped teasingly down again, then it was his turn to grasp her small, firm buttocks and lift her. She wanted to ride him forever like this..

But all Lorne could focus on was he was bending her back on to the bed as he finally lost control. . . Neither had she any control of her own wild feelings. That had gone the first moment she had felt his body pressed against hers.

Every past minute with Shane had been Heaven; this was more. She had been so long without him. Every part of her cried out for more and more. Through half-closed eyes she saw him, fully aroused, erect, beautiful.

Then, like a flash of light, Lorne was remembering every wonderful intimate moment they'd ever shared, but she'd

43

forgotten how sweet they'd been. He looked marvellous. Body taut, well-muscled, athletic, illuminated by his passion. He was amazing. And his eyes caressed her. Everywhere.

Shane smiled as he stroked back her hair. He kissed it, buried his face in it and she shivered in ecstasy. He put his mouth against her ear, his tongue flicking in and out, bringing her wild, little shocks of startled sweetness in places Lorne never thought existed. All her imaginings of him since they'd parted had just been pale shadows.

As he continued to kiss her ears, he was pushing one of her hands down, guiding to place it - she gasped with pleasure as she felt his hardness. She stroked and caressed him as he took her other hand and twined it in his.

"Oh, Lorne," he murmured, his voice thick with emotion. Next he was caressing and fondling her breasts, his mouth sweet and hard bringing her to another ecstasy of pleasure. For one brief moment, she was thinking about the past and then she drove the thought from her head.

"Shane, Shane," she ached under his kisses, but she wanted more and more.

"My love," he said softly as his lips moved down and down, kissing every nerve line and sinew, driving her into a frenzy. Her body tightened as his tongue hit her pleasure spot, sending sharp, wonderful sensations throughout her body. She writhed beneath him, twining her fingers in the dark mane of his hair . . .

As he brought his head up from between her thighs, roved on up her body, she cried out with delight. Then her heart lurched as she felt him surging into her, deep inside for his pleasure and hers.

"Shane, oh, Shane!" was all she could murmur. It had only been him. Always. Forever. Lorne brought her thighs

44

together strongly, held him, felt every part of him respond.

And he drove on deep, his back arching. Lorne clung on to his neck, begging for more, her mouth searching for his and he bent and gave it to her. She took his tongue deep and savoured it. They were almost there . . .

"Darling, darling." Then he gave her back his mouth and they plunged on in unison. Lorne drew him inside her. In her head, she held Shane body and soul, taking her life from him.

Their bodies were complete; halves, locked, welded, melting into each other. They could do anything, feel everything. They were one.

"Now, Shane, now!" she cried out and a white-hot explosion filled her. This is what dying would be. But of pleasure. It was all Lorne could think of. All she remembered of the world. Her shattering orgasm made everything into nothing except relief and warmth as they went over the edge together into ecstasy . . .

* * *

Neither of them spoke but just lay, exhausted. It seemed like hours until Shane moved beside her. Then taking her in his protecting arms, he said gently:

"Now you know, Lorne, how much I needed you."

"Yes," she shivered, cuddling against him. It was all she could trust herself to say. She could still make no sense of anything as she drifted away into comforting sleep.

Later she woke briefly, then slept again, cuddled into him. She didn't know if he was asleep but his eyes were closed. She reached up and kissed the lids. He opened those startling dark eyes. She could hardly understand the expression she saw there.

"Shane," she whispered, coming to. She looked across

45

to the window where the dawn had broken into full daylight, "I'm going to run the bath."

"Okay," he said. She knew by his tone he was fully awake. Just as she was gathering the sheet about her, he put out his hand to stop her. She turned.

"Is something the matter?" He shook his head.

"It was wonderful, Lorne. I'd forgotten just how wonderful. It was so good." He smiled and she smiled back. "Remember, Lorne, I need you. I always have. *Whatever happens.*" She nodded.

"I know, Shane." She was happy with what he said, with what they'd done but, as she crossed the room with him still watching her, she was thinking about his last sentence.

But Lorne wasn't going to let it worry her. She wasn't prepared to think of anything unpleasant just then. She just wanted to savour those precious, precious moments.

* * *

Lorne ran a very deep bath. The expensive, scented liquid she poured in afterwards changed the water into a drifting, fragrant mass of airy bubbles.

She lay there comfortably, fulfilled, the silky water lapping about the breasts he'd caressed so skilfully. She smoothed her body all over imagining he was touching her again . . .

The water was reviving her sated senses. She looked across to the door. She wished he would come in and get in the bath with her. Then they could make love again. She glowed at the memory. They'd made love in the water before. . .

It had been a cold afternoon but she and Shane had still made for the hidden cove which could be reached only by motor boat. Even though that day was a very choppy

46

crossing, Shane knew his home coastline so well and the cove was their favourite place to make love.

It was nearly always deserted, even in summer and the protecting cliffs made their presence hardly obvious from anyone silly enough to venture standing on the cliff top or sailing out at sea on that wild early Spring day.

The fine sand was white, firm and untouched until their bodies pressed into it frenziedly, scoring the deep marks of their passion. It had been so marvellous making love that they hadn't even cared about the weather. Looking back, there were things Lorne didn't want to remember after they parted. But that one time was carved on her heart.

It had seemed that the natural world around them had been set on fire by their burning bodies. Sand, sky and angry sea were all Lorne could remember as they lay, wrapped together in their anoraks, against the granite warmth of protecting rock.

It was then Lorne had begged him mischievously, seductively, "The noise of the sea's driving me mad inside." And he'd given her that wide, wry, boyish grin, which had disappeared now for ever.

They'd dashed like mad things on to the edge of the strand and let their toes be touched by the trails of the grey-white, freezing, cold rollers. Then they'd run back to the warmth of the stones and had fallen on top of each other, laughing and shrieking, crazy with love for each other, from loving each other - and, later, they'd huddled by the protecting boulders and made love even more with the waves crashing not far from them.

Above the grey sky had an almost blue smile and the tremulous early Spring sun had added its warmth to their burning skin; while the mighty waves reflected their passion and their heartbeats with a thunderous response..

47

"It was so wonderful that time, Shane," Lorne murmured, soaping her breasts; the nipples already standing out as she remembered, "and we didn't think of anything then. But now . . ." she broke off, swallowing. She didn't really want to reprise the outcome of that reckless, delirious day in their lives . . .

"Shane," she called, suddenly wanting to be comforted. Sooner or later, they would have to discuss the past, however painful. And she had to tell him what she'd been through . . ."Shane?" The rainbow bubbles were bursting around her. "Will you come here? Please?" She could hear the seductive tone in her voice, but he didn't reply.

Lorne waited. It seemed like eternity. Then, puzzled, she stretched out of the bubbled fragrance and reached for the towel sheet. Stepping out of the bath, she dried herself and wound it about her.

As she came out of the steaming bathroom into the white bedroom, she went terribly cold. "No. God, no. Shane? Shane? Where are you?" She put a hand to her mouth.

He had gone. There was no reply from anywhere. There was a space in her bed where his body had been. She couldn't understand. Her wild eyes roved round the room. Every trace of him was gone.

He'd left her. She ran across the living room into her small hall. Shirt, tie, everything. Gone. The white ceramic tiles reflected her misery clinically. *Shane had gone.* After what they'd done, he'd upped and left her without even saying goodbye. She couldn't believe it.

Stumbling back into the living area, Lorne collapsed on a chair by the table and, putting her head down, she felt the cold marble top pressing against her skull.

And, suddenly, crying was bursting out of her. She shouted and swore, letting herself go hysterically. Shane had *used* her. *Used* her - like before. All over again. How

48

could he do it? How could she have been so *stupid*?

Then she was remembering the look in his eyes and his words. *Whatever happens it was good. Remember, Lorne, I need you. Whatever happens.* He must have planned to leave even then. She didn't understand.

Lorne rocked to and fro in her misery. Finally, when she came to, she pulled up the towel which had slipped off her naked body and walked slowly into the bedroom. The intense misery and disappointment she was feeling made her look away from her own bed. She couldn't bear to lie down where they'd made love. So, dragging off the sheet, she doubled it and wrapped it about her shivering body. Then Lorne crouched on her easy chair and closed her eyes in exhaustion against the brightness of the day outside.

It was at that moment she knew the dream which had been full of so much sweetness had turned into a familiar nightmare, where her worst fears about ever meeting Shane Westonman again, had truly been confirmed.

* * *

She was woken by the insistent ring of the telephone. Cramped and cold in that sultry tropical morning, she crawled stiffly over just to shut it up. The voice which cracked in her ear was urgently insistent:

"Lorne. What the hell's happened? Are you still sick? Answer me." Lance. Ironic. She had to moisten her dry lips to let the word come out.

"No," she lied, lifting her head, looking at the bed and away again. Then she swallowed and shook herself into life. But she was sicker than she'd ever been.

"You're sleepy," he accused. Lorne's eyes were closed. Over there - in that bed - she and Shane had made love

- had sex - whatever - and he'd walked out on her. . .

"You're sure you're all right?" She was silent, which he must have taken for acquiescence. "Good. Now - hold on to your hat - are you ready for this? A surprise?"

"What?" she snapped. Why the hell couldn't he get off the phone? She wasn't in the mood for his cheerfulness.

"I told you last night. Remember? Lorne, are you there?" The tone was changing quickly into irritability.

"Yes."

"You need to get some gear together."

"Why?"

"You're still asleep," he exploded. His anger hit home. Lorne pulled herself together. "We're flying out. England. Today. This afternoon."

"England? Who is?"

"We are. The four of us. You, me, Westonman and his girlfriend."

"*Them*!" Lorne couldn't take it in.

"And us." He was being patient now. "By the way, you ought to get to know Moyra. She's one hell of a woman. You two would get on." Lorne nearly threw up. She swallowed to calm herself.

"Shane is going to England?"

"Yes, honey. He's invited us to look over one of his most successful projects. North Cornish coast, he says. Search me where that is. Do you know?" She didn't answer. "In his private jet, honey. How about that? Just a couple of days. And it'll do you good. The break. Now, doesn't *that* cheer you up?" He was waiting.

"Yes," she muttered ungraciously, which he would take for irritability. He knew she wasn't much good in the morning. *But there was no way she was going with Shane.*

"Right, I'll send the limo round at two. Got it? Sure?"

"I don't want to go," she said. There was silence.

50

"What?"

"I just don't. I don't feel well."

"For Christ's sake, Lorne, pull yourself together. It was only a few oysters. And there'll be a doc over there, if you need one. *I* need you anyway and don't say another word. You're going or - sure as hell - you're fired." Lance was in one hell of a strop and she didn't blame him.

"Okay," she said, giving in. She didn't want to lose her job, especially now. And Lance had been good to her. "All right, all right, I'll go. Now get off the phone, damn you!"

"Good. That's more like it. You must be getting better." She heard him laughing and thought just what an asshole he could be sometimes. Lorne smashed down the receiver, staggered over to the bed and lay face down, pummelling the mattress in frustration.

It was all a nightmare. She'd loved Shane and lost him - again and again. *He was a shit*. But she loved him. That was a fact. What they'd done together had been mind-blowing. *And she still wanted him*. So how could she call him that? She loved him. And those words of his were drumming in her head. *Remember it was good. Whatever happens, remember it was good.*

Lorne buried her head in the pillow where his had been. She was going crazy. Then she grabbed at her watch. Squinted at the small face. Ten o'clock already. *In the morning*.

She jumped up in panic. *Two o'clock. England.* What the hell was she going to do? What should she take with her? She had to get ready. But she couldn't bear to go. What would happen if she didn't turn up at the airport again?

* * *

51

CHAPTER 4

The powerful hum of the jet's engines should have sent Lorne off to sleep. But she and Shane never closed their eyes.

Lance's were shut although he'd been reading through the project plans earlier. Now, he was seated beside Moyra, who was resting, eyes closed, her neck supported by a pillow. On her lap lay copies of *Vogue*, *Harpers & Queens* and *Country Living*. She was dressed casually but the total effect had probably cost Shane at least a thousand dollars.

Lorne had no illusions as to how Moyra worked. The girl would use him unmercifully. And then Lorne thought of what had happened between her and Shane that morning. Their present bizarre situation was getting to her. She'd agreed to this trip only because she had no option.

She was full of restless recriminations. She only trusted herself to glance at Shane when she was sure he wouldn't notice. He was sitting directly opposite her.

Earlier, he'd gone over the plans with Lance. In fact, the men had begun working immediately after take-off; the discussions hadn't been Lorne's field - too technical - which had put her into the awkward position of having to make conversation with Moyra.

It had been such a pain, but the girl had evidently disliked it as much as Lorne. She must have been well briefed by Shane because never once did she refer to the past or even show that she and Lorne had ever been acquainted.

Eventually the two of them found there was nothing else to say to each other. They had run out of small talk and, as Moyra had had her orders, there was no open hostility. Finally, Moyra turned back to her magazines and deliberately began to read, ignoring Lorne . . .

When Shane sat down opposite her, it was a dreadful moment. Boarding the plane, he'd greeted her with a brief kiss on both cheeks. Bearing that had taken all Lorne's self-control. Yet she'd smiled brightly and given him "Good afternoon, Shane" in response. Why the hell had she got herself into this mess?

Shane stretched out his long legs, settling himself. He was wearing an immaculate beige suit, made out of fine wool in preparation for the cool English summer.

He was starting to flick through *The Financial Times*. A silver coffee set, the tray covered with a finely embroidered white cloth had been brought to him a few minutes earlier. Lorne had pretended to be asleep just in case he asked her to join him. It was a necessary ploy. She would have gone crazy having to make small talk to *him*.

She continued to feign sleep, having made sure her legs were crossed carefully. She turned side on to him slightly so he couldn't see her expression, but she was watching him through half-closed lids.

As Shane stretched out his hand and poured himself some coffee into the pretty porcelain cup, a sharp pang shot through her. She watched him drinking, thought of his mouth kissing hers, his body against hers - biting her lip, Lorne breathed in deeply and completely closed her eyes, letting herself hide behind them.

How could one man cause so much pain? She'd been so indiscreet. She'd let him carry on where he'd left off. She shouldn't have let him make love to her last night.

If she'd sent him away, kept the whole world she'd created as a defence around her, she would still have something to hope for. For instance, this trip. If they hadn't made love, she'd be able to imagine they might - one day, once more. Now she felt cheated again. She was paying for another serious indiscretion. Again.

She opened her eyes. *You stupid fool*, she said to herself, as a streak of cloud like white candy floss floated by the plane's porthole. They must be descending. Caught off guard, she jumped as she heard Shane say:

"You're awake then? Lorne?" She didn't answer. Didn't he understand she didn't want to talk to him? That she felt drained mentally and physically. "Then we can talk?" She opened her eyes wide and stared at him. She didn't understand either what was in that dark look which held hers unswervingly. But she couldn't say a thing to him. It was his place to explain.

If she didn't know him, love him in spite of everything, she would have said he was an unfeeling bastard. Suddenly, in Lorne's opinion, he was confirming her unspoken accusation as he added off-handedly, "I suggest you relax. We've a busy schedule ahead." And that was the end of a one-way conversation. He didn't speak to her again.

It was only when she was getting off the plane, watching Shane jump down the few steps in front of her, she had cooled down enough to admit to herself that any personal discussion in the plane's cabin would have been unthinkable. Whereas at the moment, Lorne's heart ruled her head, Shane was just the opposite.

* * *

Lorne looked out of the window across the moor. She hadn't been home for ages. Although *home* meant London, England and her parents, in her heart it had meant Cornwall and Shane. He drove expertly with Moyra beside him in the front passenger seat.

Yet his frequent glances in the driving mirror had resulted in his eyes meeting Lorne's quickly several times. But she'd avoided their contact, swiftly turning to the window and the miles of heather and gorse as the Rolls Royce cruised silently along the snake-like road across Bodmin Moor.

Wearing the beige suit had been the right choice as usual. Cornwall was windswept today and wet. She could smell the familiar scent of England even through the air conditioning. It was an exhilarating difference from the sandy heat of the Canaries. But Lorne was feeling too strung-up, too much on edge to enjoy anything. The grandeur of the gloomy landscape suited her mood.

However Lance didn't find her moodiness contagious. He was spending a lot of the journey leaning over the front seat, laughing and joking with Moyra who kept turning her elegant head to him. They seemed to be getting on very well.

On the other hand, Shane's silence was brooding, ominous, stern. Lorne had never managed to drive one picture of him out of her mind. She had kept it there to remind her of both the sad and lovely times she'd spent in beautiful Cornwall. . . Shane, standing high on the edge of the cliffs, dark hair tousled by the wind, coat collar up, a romantic hero, a real Heathcliff. Yes, today, Shane was like that. . .

"Nearly home, darling," quipped Moyra.

Her home and his. A stab of jealous pain shot through Lorne as she thought of Shane and her together. And that must be an engagement ring Moyra was wearing. She supposed they'd already planned the wedding given the circumstances.

Lance had filled her in on the details he thought she ought to know, while they were waiting at the airport. What would he think if she told him she knew everything about the two of them already. She had no option but to listen and look interested. And if only he'd known what she'd done with Moyra's precious fiancé last night.

But something inside her wanted to find out the kind of lifestyle Shane was enjoying now. She could have guessed though.

"Now, listen, honey, this deal might come off but Westonman Associates have a lot of other projects in the pipeline. They could be very useful to us. To me and my business. Why do you think we're really going on this trip?" She had answered briefly:

"To look over one of his pet projects, I suppose."

"Right. A completed one. Now what does that tell you?" She shook her head. Right then, playing guessing games with Lance was beyond her. But her boss was regarding her doubtfully. She could see he was thinking she was still ill. He added, "Do you think you're going to be okay on the trip?"

"I told you I wasn't well," she said, glad of the excuse. At lunchtime, she'd decided anything would have been better than going but, an hour later, she'd been on her way to the airport in the limo. Her emotions had been telling her then that perhaps Shane Westonman had an explanation for his extraordinarily cruel action. But her head was telling her there wasn't one.

And listening to Lance going on about the business, she'd realised the American had the impression that Denver Inc. had pushed right through the ceiling, had made the breakthrough he'd been waiting for and finally made it to number one with Westonman Associates. Knowing Shane as she did, Lorne wasn't so sure.

Lance's sharp eyes were sparkling when he said, "I told the guy about the plans I have for the hotel complex in Sardinia, and he's showing an interest already. And what about this? The guy actually knows the Aga Khan personally. And . . ." Lance paused, ready to deliver the final bombshell. ". . . he can pull strings with NATO. The guy's a business legend. We are really on the way, honey. Westonman in on the hook." And Lance had rubbed his hands in anticipation, adding: "You see, honey, that's why I wanted you along. The guy likes you a lot."

"Why do you say that?" she had asked sharply.

"Because he keeps talking about you."

"Why? What does he say?"

"The usual. I can tell when someone has the hots."

"What do you mean?" Lance was grinning.

"Take it easy. Nothing like that. I was kidding. Anyway, you're my girl."

"Am I?"

"You know you are." She had turned away deliberately and looked at the aircraft. What a mess she was in. Lance had no right to call her his *girl*. She wasn't and he knew it, but she hadn't the strength to fight him then.

As for Shane talking about her - what had he said? How could he after what they'd done? And what would Lance have thought if he'd known how much she'd done for Denver Inc. already? He'd probably have been over the moon, *his girl* or not. If it meant cash in the bank. But that was bitter, wasn't it . . ?

Lorne smiled ruefully. But she just kept staring across the moor as it flashed by. She wondered what this new place of Shane's was like. She supposed it was just another base adding to his estates in Bermuda and the States.

She was up to here with it all. Impatiently, Lorne stretched up and unclasped the fine-silver collar she was wearing. It seemed like it was strangling her. Lance had given it to her and it perfectly complemented the blue business suit. Shane had seen the move.

"You okay in the back?" Moyra glanced across at Shane quickly.

"Great," answered Lance. "Scenery sure beats those miserable islands. What do you say, Lorne?" Her boss was certainly taking every opportunity to ingratiate himself. She wasn't surprised when Shane's amused eyes flicked away. He'd always been astute, seen through obvious insincerity, was impervious to flattery.

She had to say something; show she wasn't as slimy as Lance.

"I wouldn't say that, Lance," she flashed, "I've had my moments over there." Lance's jaw dropped, his narrow green eyes widening with surprise. It always annoyed him when he was contradicted. But she didn't care about Lance. Lorne had only said it for Shane's benefit.

He was looking in the mirror again and that intimate hint of smiling humour was still in his dark eyes. Then he concentrated on the road again. Lorne bristled. So he found her amusing as well? She tingled with resentment at the injustice. It was no laughing matter.

She leaned back against the luxurious leather seat, feeling miserable again. Suddenly Moyra was turning. Then she placed one hand lightly on Lance's knee. Her long fingers were beautifully manicured and finished with scarlet varnish. The lovely rings she wore on every finger flashed in the sunlight.

"There it is, Lance, down there. Our complex." Her

perfect, pouting mouth had arched into a tiny smile. Lorne knew instinctively that her attention to Lance was tit for tat for Lorne's with Shane.

It was a trivial gesture but Lorne was beginning to realise what she'd suspected through the whole of the journey. Moyra was taking more than just an ordinary interest in her boss.

She hadn't changed. But she had Shane where she wanted him. Lorne had always sensed Moyra could never be faithful whatever the circumstances; would never make Shane happy however much he was bound to her and, of course, Lance would play up to it.

Shane's eyes didn't miss Moyra's move. She saw him flick her one glance, then return to the road. And Moyra was leaving her hand there. Lorne watched Lance smile back at her. But Shane didn't look angry. He just ignored the gesture, driving on relentlessly.

Just what kind of relationship do you have with Moyra, Shane? How can you bear living like this? But she supposed he had to. He would be loyal. Yet why hadn't he been loyal to her? Perhaps he would have if Lorne had told him the truth? But she didn't want him to have to choose. She couldn't make him. And she'd lost him.

On that painful journey, Lorne asked Shane so many questions from deep in her heart. And, as the car rolled on down the winding road towards the bay, suddenly the sun broke through the dark clouds.

* * *

The following morning was just as bright. Lorne was sitting in the foyer of Shane's sumptuous hotel.

"Good morning." One of the early-morning risers acknowledged her on her way to the fitness centre and pool entrance in the corner. A moment later, Lorne was extremely surprised to see Lance emerge. He had a towel draped round his shoulders and was wearing black tee shirt and shorts. He'd evidently been early morning swimming.

His hair was slick and wet and, for the thousandth time in her life, she thought how annoying Lance could be. He was almost bouncing along, grinning to himself. He stopped to check how he looked in the long mirror placed at the entrance to the gym.

Then he caught sight of Lorne and waved. Next moment, he was coming over to where she was sitting looking at the morning papers. Somehow, she hadn't thought he'd be exercising that morning after his late night.

She was sure that their dinner for four last night hadn't ended very early for Lance. She knew the signs. It hadn't take her long to leave the table. She hadn't fancied playing gooseberry to a voluble Lance and Moyra who hung on his every word.

Although Lorne had been dreading an intimate foursome dinner with Shane and Moyra, it hadn't worked out too badly after all.

Besides, Shane had been called away after three quarters of an hour or so and Lorne had been both happy and sad to see him go. It had given her the chance to get off the bed. The last thing she felt like was trivial conversation. So she'd taken a rain-check herself.

Wherever Shane had gone, it had kept him away all evening. And Reception had a message from him this morning, for herself and Lance - saying he was sorry but he'd been unavoidably detained and hoped to return for lunch . . .

"Hi, honey." Lance's green eyes sparkled.

"You look pleased with yourself," Lorne said, looking up from *The Times*. If she'd said that three days ago he'd have taken it as a come-on. Now he had other things on his mind. She wondered wryly if his bed had been slept in.

"You, too, honey. Gee, that colour suits you."

"Thank you," she replied coldly. Lorne was a strawberry blonde naturally. It was only the sun which bleached her hair. Her colours were cool but soft. She knew that this morning her dark-blue eyes seemed startlingly deep and clear because they were heightened by the ice-pink shirt.

"I'll just go and get dressed. Great swim. Great morning." Lance grinned again. "See you later. Bye." She nodded. He was certainly in a good mood. She watched him stride off, quite sure she was right about him and Moyra.

What *did* Shane think of the way Moyra was behaving? Somehow she couldn't imagine him approving. Lorne put down the newspaper and closed her eyes briefly. His going along with Moyra's behaviour was probably something to do with her family - or his.

Lorne swallowed, remembering. When Shane said he needed her, she didn't know she was going to be a pawn in some game he was still playing with Moyra Trevise. But he'd behaved as if he *loved* her . . . Lorne went over what had happened for the hundredth time since Shane had walked out of her bedroom without any explanation.

She'd always know about his reputation but, somehow, she'd always believed he'd change - *with the right girl*. And Lorne had never thought Moyra was. She might be a fitting ornament for Shane's home; she had the looks and the background. But she was cold and ruthless. Lorne knew that from experience. And, above all, calculating.

But where was the evidence? How could she find out? Lorne opened her eyes and picked up a magazine, flipping through it in a totally disinterested way. Her

61

mind was in one place only. Shane. He could be cold as well. He was astute. Perhaps that was the same as *calculating*?

Lorne gave up thinking about it. She'd been fair competition for Moyra once; but her rival had won the prize. Lorne was human, after all. Who wouldn't want to own a complex like this? It was fabulous.

But *live* in it? No, that wouldn't be her choice. If she'd had Shane she would have wanted to rush away with him to some glorious, secret place where he could cosset and care for her.

You are a fool, Lorne, she said to herself, *you're still dreaming about him. After all he's done to you. You'll never learn. If you and Shane were still together, he'd be rushing all over the world anyway and leaving you behind.*

Shane was the supreme businessman and never happier when he was planning some new project or big deal. It was just Lorne's love for him which kept getting in the way of reason. *No, she'd never learn.* That was what her mother had said on that terrible day she'd gone back home from Cornwall and told them what had happened between her and Shane. She could hear her mother's voice. "I just don't know how you can defend him." It had been so painful, but she couldn't keep the secret much longer. And they'd supported her as she knew they would . . .

Lorne sighed, looking round the foyer. Whatever had happened didn't matter now. It was too late. She'd almost made her mind up what to do this morning with Shane away.

Before dinner last night he'd hiked her and Lance all round the complex. He was merciless, discussing with Lance all the technicalities and architectural jargon. But, occasionally, she'd seen flashes of sympathy for her in his eyes.

62

He wouldn't be back until lunchtime so she should take the opportunity while Lance was off her back too. He was well-known for kicking-up a fuss about wasting good business time.

However, his preoccupation with Moyra had signalled a change in attitude - for a while at least. So she'd make the most of it. Lorne replaced the unread magazine on the pile and, yawning, walked over to the window.

No wonder her heart ached for Shane. Everything about the landscape reminded her of happier days. The vast expanse of windows he had created, exposed wide lawns sweeping to the very edge of the cliffs. Pure parkland drawn from the barren heart of the shore, yet blending in, broken only by sweet-fragranced acres of borders and a huge variety of unusual trees.

Just looking at such beauty helped Lorne make up her mind. She walked over to the smiling girl manning Reception.

"Do you have a map of the area, please?" She wanted to make sure. She'd also have to hire a car. If she was remembering right, it was only about an hour's drive to Westonman village from where she was now.

She was going to ring Jane first. They hadn't kept in touch, although they'd promised to. But Jane was the kind of person you could just drop in on. It was Lorne's fault. She hadn't written to anyone in Cornwall. She'd just cut herself off from her old life. She wanted it that way. At least, that's what she'd been telling herself until she met Shane again.

But, in the light of what had suddenly happened between them, Lorne was determined to find out if what Moyra Trevise had told her was the whole truth. It seemed to be, but things didn't fit now somehow.

Lorne's mind flicked to the clusters of wonderful

63

diamond rings Moyra wore on her fingers. Had Shane given her one of them? Were they really engaged? Lorne just didn't know and who else could she ask but Jane.

If it hadn't been for what Moyra told her, Lorne wouldn't have given up so easily. And, if she hadn't, then she felt sure she mightn't have gone through what she finally did on her own.

* * *

Lorne lay on her bed, telephone poised. "Jane?" The line crackled. Her friend's voice sounded distant, unrecognisable.

"Who is it?" Evidently Jane didn't recognise her either but, when she suddenly did, the doctor's wife could hardly believe it. "Of course you can come over. I'd love to see you. Wonderful. I can't wait."

Hiring the car was easy. She didn't need to. Shane had left orders that his guests should have absolutely anything they needed - transport included. Not the Rolls, but a Mercedes Coupe.

Lorne was delighted. She was used to scrappy little cars on the island - except for Lance's limo, of course. The red hubs of the car glinted in the sun. "Okay, I can handle it now, thank you." She dismissed the man who brought it round from the garage after he'd showed her the controls. She was in a hurry and the car was no problem: It was an automatic and, anyway, she was used to driving everything and anything in Lanzarote.

But once inside, seated at the white leather-covered wheel, she found herself excited about driving it. Lorne had always liked fast, stylish cars. "Beautiful," she murmured, sliding the automatic gear lever into the start mode.

She'd hardly pressed the accelerator and moved off when she was suddenly forced to make an emergency stop. "What the hell is the fool doing?" She caught her breath sharply and jammed the lever into Park.

The huge horse, sun shining on its chestnut flanks had come careering round the narrow bend in the hotel drive. The animal was lathered all over and had evidently been ridden hard. It towered over the car as the rider wheeled its head round.

Lorne ducked involuntarily, made a face in annoyance, pulled up the sun visor and squinted angrily as the electric window slid down.

"You might be more careful," she shouted. "I nearly ran into you." The man was already out of the saddle. She could hear his boots scrunching on the gravel as he tried to calm the plunging animal. Lorne waited for the outburst. Then *Shane's* face appeared at the car window. Lorne gasped.

"Did you expect me to honk my horn?" he replied sarcastically. "Now who's a bad driver?" he was referring to their very first meeting. Lorne bristled, stiffened. But the humorous sarcasm in his tone didn't match the expression in his eyes. They were dark and angry.

He was being so unfair. He didn't like her shouting at him but he was prepared to shout at her.

"I am not," she said, leaning back. "it was your fault. And it was a good thing I didn't honk my horn. It might have thrown you." There was one silent moment. It gave them both time to cool off. Then she heard him laugh.

Her eyes were level with his waist as he stood there, the horse skittering behind him. She noted the expensive belt and flamboyant silver buckle - the wonderfully-cut jodhpurs.

A moment later, she was looking up at him. He'd

controlled his temper. Then he took off his hard hat and the strong breeze was ruffling the black wings of his hair, tossing a few floppy strands over his eyes.

With a lithe movement, he swept it back and her heart lurched. It was another gesture she'd never forgotten. She was suddenly remembering how he'd stroked back her hair when they'd made love.

His riding jacket with the velvet collar fitted his strong body perfectly, while the pure, white polo-neck sweater he wore beneath showed off his tan even more. Lorne swallowed thinking about his body . . .

He looked into her eyes. "I was just in time then. Running off again?"

Her heart thumped. Not only with excitement but because of his insensitivity. "I'm not the one who's running off," she said. "Any objection? The message said you'd be out until lunch." She knew there was an edge to her voice. She couldn't help it. Besides, the near miss had frightened her.

Suddenly she didn't want to spar with Shane any more. She was weary with it all. Why couldn't things have gone right for a change? And, all the time, his keen eyes were searching her face.

"Don't worry, Lorne, I've no intention of spoiling your outing." He straightened up. "Go where you like." What arrogance. She was going to anyway.

"I will." Didn't he realise how much he'd hurt her? In every way.

"Memory Lane, I suppose." He could be so flippant. And cruel. But, she *had* snapped at him. And he was always so proud. Always had found it difficult to climb down. But making-up with Shane was Heaven.

Suddenly, his fingers drummed on the soft top of the Mercedes. "Good luck then." She took it as a curt dismissal.

"Right." Lorne shot the Mercedes into Start and Shane had to jump back quickly. Next moment, she was rounding the bend but, as she glanced in the mirror, she saw him standing motionless, just watching her.

* * *

CHAPTER 5

Lorne asked herself lots of questions about Shane on that drive to Westonman village. And found no answers. He'd always been unpredictable, but to leave dinner last night? Disappear? Send a message to say he wouldn't be back until lunch time? Then, given how short their stay was, go out riding before ten o'clock in the morning as if he had all the time in the world.

Had he been away from the hotel all night? But it was only Moyra who knew that? Or Lance? Lorne concluded that this was outrageous behaviour. Even for Shane.

As she drove the company Mercedes along the lanes, she was too afraid to flatter herself his behaviour might have anything to do with her. Shane had always done as he pleased and would continue to do so.

That's probably the answer, Lorne told herself as she slowed down purposefully, thrilling to the view.

Familiar ground - at last. In the distance, the woods, surrounding Seaview School, looked just the same. Below, the houses in the village were huddled together to protect themselves from the worst of the weather blowing in from the coast and, to the right, was the three-mile long deserted beach, where she and Shane had walked and talked through those heady days which seemed so long ago.

Lorne felt like a time-traveller as she looked at the view; as if nothing had changed. But, she was deluding herself, everything had.

The spell was broken. Deliberately, she pressed the accelerator and the car moved off down the hill. At the same time, she was asking herself why the hell had she decided to come back to Westonman, when she'd promised herself she'd never return, even though her life depended on it. . .

* * *

"Lorne. It's wonderful to see you again after all this time," cried Jane. She looked so capable, just like a busy doctor's wife had to be in a small-town practice. Everyone called on Jane for help and she gave it wholeheartedly.

"And you." Lorne and she hugged each other on the step.

"Come on inside." Jane's keen eyes were taking in Lorne's strained look. "You've timed it nicely. I've just made some coffee." Then her gaze held Lorne's.

"What's that look for?" Lorne smiled.

"You're thinner," accused Jane.

"Hardly surprising," retorted Lorne. "It's hot in the Canaries."

"I didn't mean that. You look - fragile."

"Is that a medical opinion? Honestly, I'm okay." She followed Jane down the hall.

"I hope you don't mind having coffee in here but the daily help's doing through the lounge and the surgery," apologised her friend.

"Of course not. I hope you don't mind, but I was near and . . ." They reached the kitchen. She looked round. " . . . you've decorated."

69

"I hope so. After all this time."

They laughed. The months seemed to slip away as Lorne sat down on one of the two comfortable old armchairs which Jane had positioned in the corner of the large dining area. It was all so different from the white decor of Lorne's little flat on the island. In fact, she'd never realised until now how different nor how indeed she'd ever got used to leaving Westonman village.

There was still the smell of something good cooking, lasagne or roast beef or pork. And the scrubbed elm of the large old table seemed friendly and welcoming. It felt like home.

As Jane was pouring the coffee, Lorne watched her. Jane was no different; capable as ever but, suddenly, Lorne had the strangest feeling of *déja vu.*

It was just every time she and Jane had sat drinking coffee, and Lorne had opened up to her - Lorne swallowed. Shane was right. Perhaps it hadn't been a good idea to walk down 'Memory Lane' again?

She couldn't help sighing. Jane handed her a cup:

"Something's the matter, isn't it? After you went back to London it was months before I heard a word from you. And afterwards nothing until - but I won't go over that news you sent. Then, here you are sitting in my lounge. Just like we used to. What's happened, Lorne?" Lorne shook her head.

"I'm sorry, Jane. I should have been in touch. But I was depressed." Jane nodded.

"I understand. We were both really worried. And John did his best, you know."

"I know. You both did. But, I told you, I'm okay now. Just visiting." She sipped the hot liquid. She found her fingers shaking a little. Jane had an intent look on her face.

"I'm sorry, but I don't believe you. You've come back to see *him*, haven't you? Haven't you, Lorne? Admit it."

It was then that Lorne made the decision not to tell Jane she'd met Shane already. Maybe she'd learn more that way. It wasn't really fair but, how did the saying go, *All's fair in love and war*. It was her love for Shane and it had been open war with Moyra.

But, again, what was the point? The two of them were together and Lorne had lost. Yet, it was Shane himself who had said, "There's always a point."

She hadn't been able to control herself the night Shane came to her flat, any more than he had. And she hadn't wanted to. Yet she'd always thought it taboo to sleep with a man who belonged to someone else. She was so confused.

She came to with a start. Jane looked as though she knew the answer. "I'm right, aren't I?"

"No, I haven't come to see him. Only to ask about how he's going on." That, at least, was the truth. "I'm here in Cornwall on business with my boss. I had to come to Westonman, seeing I was close." Would Jane swallow it? Evidently. Her old friend was smiling.

"I'm glad you did. I missed you such a lot after you left. We had some good times." Lorne nodded, looking round the room.

"I had to come back, Jane. I was happy here, really."

"By the look on your face now, I'd never have guessed," said Jane bluntly. "And, I'm afraid you won't be seeing Shane. He's abroad."

Lorne managed to look sorry about it. "Any more bad news?" It was the most flippant remark she could manage. To think she'd been as close to Shane as ever she had; and she went on deceiving her friend.

"You're your own worst enemy, Lorne. It won't do you

71

any good to see him." Jane was stirring her coffee briskly.

"Won't it?" Lorne asked, then added, "Maybe I have to."

"You still care about him, don't you? In spite of what happened?" Lorne nodded.

"Yes. How's he getting on?" She had to know what had happened since she left. If what Moyra had told her was true? Lorne didn't need a psychologist to tell her that Jane had been dreading the question. She looked more awkward than ever Lorne had seen her as she sipped the coffee.

"Oh, that's hot." She found the courage. "This might be a bit of a shock but Shane got engaged when you left."

Lorne was sorry for putting Jane in that position. Yet, all she could say was, "Oh," looking as surprised as she could at the same time. There was silence, then Jane added, "I can't think why though. They live seperate lives."

"Do they?" Lorne's instincts had been good again. But then why were they still travelling about together?

"You don't seem bothered?" said Jane quietly.

"Why should I be? I knew they'd marry some time," replied Lorne.

"But they haven't. Perhaps they won't? Shane and Moyra have similar business interests even though they're apart most of the time. But I don't think it was ever a proper engagement. In fact, I don't think they'll ever marry." Jane was staring at Lorne very hard with an *I-told-you-so* look on her face.

"You mean it's just a convenience?" Lorne's heart was beating very fast.

"I suppose so. We were surprised, Lorne, we really were . . ." Jane broke off. Then, suddenly, she stretched out her hand and clasped Lorne's in a sympathetic gesture.

72

"Who?"

"The people who knew you and Shane. I'm sure he loved you, Lorne. But you pushed him right into Moyra's arms. And it was what she wanted. You out of the way. Don't you see that? Why did you run off like that? Why didn't you tell him?"

Suddenly Lorne had to say something. She let out a sigh of frustration. "And I was proved right, wasn't I? I went because I had to. Because of her. You don't understand, do you? You only knew half the story. I know I was a fool, but I thought I'd done the right thing. I believed Shane didn't love me - that he wanted Moyra instead. He got engaged to her, for God's sake."

Lorne hadn't meant to burst out like that. Jane just sat quietly, listening. She nodded and went on patting Lorne's hand.

"Evidently they fight like cat and dog. And somebody told me she'd been unfaithful. I never thought he'd stand for that. But, on the other hand, I heard that Moyra had some kind of hold over him."

"You don't know what?"

Jane shook her head.

Again, Lorne's heart was racing. So it wasn't true what Moyra had said on that awful night. Why had she been stupid enough to believe her?

"Oh, dear," said Jane, straightening. "John would probably tell me off for saying what I just have. After all, it isn't my business. And Moyra, as you know, *is* a distant relative of his." They looked at each other and suddenly burst out laughing, which broke the tension.

"How your husband could ever be a relation of Moyra Trevise I can't imagine," said Lorne.

"I know. It's really awful. But I shouldn't have said what I did."

73

"You can say anything about Moyra as far as I'm concerned," retorted Lorne. Jane was looking at her closely.

"I have to say this though. You've changed."

"How?"

"Well, I suppose from that girl who ran off with just a goodbye. We were worried sick and when we heard the outcome. And then you went away."

"Don't remind me about the past, Jane. I think I've grown up. I thought I had the answer to everything then. I am different, I think, but, sometimes . . ." she broke off shaking her head. She didn't want to finish the sentence, knowing that didn't include the way she felt about Shane. She was just as stupid about him now as she'd ever been.

Inside she was just as vulnerable, just as liable to take him on face value, to fall back into his arms. Hadn't she proved it over the last few days?

But there *was* a difference. And if he didn't care for Moyra any more then perhaps - Lorne forced herself not to think about it. Mentally she squashed every bit of hope she had as she looked straight at Jane.

"I know I shouldn't have come back. But, still, I ought to face it. Shane is engaged to Moyra. That's a fact whatever's wrong between them. He made a choice. He didn't come after me, did he?" It was so difficult. Of course, he hadn't, given the situation with Moyra and knowing nothing about Lorne's. But Jane didn't know the true Moyra angle.

"On the other hand, I can't just turn off the feelings I had - and still have - for him." Lorne added. Jane was nodding sympathetically.

"But, still, it's nice to be back in Westonman however I feel. Nice to know other things haven't changed. The village; you; everything looks the same."

"Only we're older - and wiser too, I hope." Jane smiled wryly. Lorne nodded, adding:

"You know I loved it here."

"I only wish I could put the clock back for you, Lorne, but with a different ending."

"We had some good times though, didn't we?" As the two of them began reminiscing, Lorne's mind switched back to the night when her troubles had really begun; the Christmas Mediaeval Ball at Seaview and her second meeting with Shane. . .

* * *

After the surprise of the twenty roses which had arrived after the near miss by the church, Lorne was involved in the main event of the school's winter calendar. It was a fund raiser, held just before Christmas in the quaint school hall, which had a mediaeval look about it with cascading pennants lighting up gloomy corners and parents and teachers in colourful fancy dress.

Lorne was feeling excited at the thought of seeing him again. She knew Shane Westonman was coming; he had to because he was a school governor and he was also giving the speech. She'd also seen his Land Rover parked outside the vicarage so he had to be home for the weekend. But it was almost ten and he was late. Lorne was dressed as Greensleeves and was trying not to dip the points of her long, awkward sleeves into the punch bowl.

"Oh, damn," she said, trying to roll them up. It was then she saw Shane striding towards her. He was the handsomest knight in the room and he made every other man look pale and insignificant.

He wasn't wearing shiny armour, but his tall,

commanding body looked wonderful in its sober, black velvet. He had a white ruffled shirt slashed open at the neck, showing the beginnings of his curly chest hair.

Lorne caught her breath as their eyes met. Then her heart was fluttering with excitement. If she'd been truthful with herself, she'd have known she was in love with Shane already. . .

"Red or white wine?" she asked, gesturing the bottles. "Or my punch?"

"Punch. If *you* made it."

"On your head be it," she joked, ladling it into the glass.

"Careful. Your sleeves are in it."

"Oh, damn," she said again and he grinned. Then, with a swift movement, he helped her to push the annoying sleeves out of the way. That brief touch made her blaze inside. She handed him the glass, smiling. He was looking in her eyes again as he raised it to his lips:

"A toast to you, Greensleeves."

"Thank you."

"You look - beautiful."

"Thanks again. You don't look too bad yourself."

"Yes, but it's hot inside here. I don't know how our ancestors managed in clothes like this." They laughed companionably and Lorne was already wondering why she'd ever thought Shane Westonman was arrogant and insensitive. . .

Later, he helped clear the hall and then walked her to her car in the winter moonlight. The clouds scudded across the midnight sky as fast as her heart beat in her ears. Then, he bent and kissed her. And that had been the beginning of it all - all Lorne wanted had been Shane - forever.

After Christmas, Shane always seemed to be at home. Lorne had spent only a few days of her Christmas holidays in London. She didn't want to be away from him, but she didn't tell her parents that. They were surprised she had to go back to Westonman so soon but she told them she had so much school work to do - new job and everything. It was selfish of her, but Lorne was very much in love.

She and Shane were meeting all the time, by accident but, most of the time, it was arranged. Two people in love - or so she believed. Lorne remembered how Jane had tried to warn her about Shane, but Lorne wouldn't have taken any notice anyway. Shane would never be seeing anyone else. Lorne trusted him implicitly.

"Be careful, Lorne," her friend had said one day as she hurried off to work, her neat, blue, nursing uniform making her look even more serious.

"What do you mean?" Lorne replied happily.

"I don't know - but Shane has - a reputation. He's always had a string of girlfriends."

"I can take care of myself, Jane," Lorne had replied confidently. She knew how other girls looked envious when they were out together, but it didn't matter. Lorne felt safe, quite indestructible in Shane's company - and things were getting serious - until Moyra turned up.

Looking back, an older and wiser Lorne knew now she should have been on her guard. . .

* * *

"You haven't heard a word I've said," accused Jane.

Lorne jumped. "Oh, I'm sorry, Jane. I'm being really rude. I was just . . ."

"Off down Memory Lane?" The phrase jolted Lorne into uncomfortable reality.

"Afraid so," she admitted. Jane nodded.

"You were thinking about Shane, weren't you? And Moyra."

"Especially her. The first time I saw her. When she came back."

"You mean after the business course?"

"Yes." It wasn't a nice thought. Lorne had come across Moyra and Shane as she was driving home from school. . .

* * *

Shane's Land Rover had been parked, facing the traffic on the opposite verge, alongside a gap in the wall, which stretched around Westonman Manor. A couple of days earlier, a car had skidded on some ice and Shane was evidently giving orders to his estate workers how he wanted it repaired.

Her heart leaped as usual when she saw him and Lorne was about to pull up when she realised that Shane was in conversation with the driver of a small, sports car which was parked up behind the Land Rover. Lorne couldn't see who was inside as she approached.

She slowed and smiled and Shane abruptly left off the conversation. Next moment he tapped on the sports's roof and, leaving the vehicle, crossed the road to Lorne. They both watched in silence as the dark-haired girl with pearl earrings switched on the powerful engine and accelerated off along the road.

Then Shane bent his head and gave Lorne a quick kiss on the cheek through the car window. She closed her eyes briefly then opened them. "Who was that, Shane?"

"Moyra Trevise. She lives round here." Lorne's heart lurched. So that was Moyra. She'd heard a lot about her.

"I've never seen her before."

"No, she's been away doing her MBA in Oxford. But -

78

it seems she's given up the course." Shane was looking in the direction the girl had gone. It was the second time Lorne had seen that look on his face. His expression wasn't angry, just thoughtful.

Whatever else, it seemed to Lorne then that Shane wasn't happy meeting Moyra Trevise in Westonman again. And she said the same to Jane. Her friend had shaken her head doubtfully, "I don't know, really I don't, Lorne. They used to go out together."

Lorne remembered the way her heart had lurched uncomfortably at the news. Jane had added, "In fact, Shane was going out with her before he met you. I know because John told me. And it was inevitable she'd come back. Of course, they've known each other since they were children. The Trevises are big noises round here. And so are the Westonmans." Jane had shrugged. "I shouldn't say this. It might upset you, Lorne . . ."

"Go on."

"Moyra's always regarded Shane as her property. She had her claws in tight."

"You don't like her much, do you?" Lorne had summed up the situation straightaway. Whenever Jane mentioned Moyra, her usually serene expression hardened. "And if Shane thought so much about her, why is he going out with me?" Lorne added stubbornly.

"Listen, love . . ." Jane was shaking her head again. "this is Westonman. The Trevises own all the land round Tregarth and Trevithick. If Shane and Moyra got together, they'd have the lot between them. See what I mean?"

"No, I don't. It sounds like the Middle Ages," retorted Lorne but, inside, she had a horrible sinking feeling. She'd never been short on confidence, but Jane's words were suddenly making her think about the competition she was facing.

But she believed in her emotions. And Shane's. She loved him and, anyway, now they were lovers, Moyra had to be out of it. . .

* * *

"Oh, dear, Lorne, you are having a bad time of it, aren't you?" remarked Jane bringing Lorne back to reality again. "Let's talk about something more cheerful. Would you like some more coffee?" Lorne shook her head.

"I really can't stay any longer," she replied. She looked at her watch. "I have to be back for lunch. Business. My boss won't forgive me if I'm late for the meeting."

"Is he nice?"

"Who?"

"The boss."

"Sometimes."

"I wish you'd stay and see John. He'll be popping in for a coffee soon." Suddenly, the door bell chimed. "That might be him now. He's probably forgotten his house key again. Absent-minded. He'll be delighted to see you. Will you excuse me a moment?"

"Sure," said Lorne. As Jane hurried out, Lorne began to collect her things . . . And then Jane was coming back into the lounge and Lorne was preparing herself to meet John again.

But in a flash Lorne knew it wasn't him because Jane's eyes were wide with warning. She turned to the tall man who was following behind her.

"*Shane*, you'll never guess who's here." Her eyes flicked and held Lorne's, who was trying to collect herself. He was still in his riding clothes. They stared at each other while Jane stood awkwardly between them. Then she said, "I'll just make some more coffee, shall I?"

"Not for me," he said. "Unless of course you and *Lorne* would like another." He said her name as if he'd never heard it before.

"No thank you, Jane," Lorne said. "Hello, Shane." He was offering his hand. She took it. "How nice to see you again." A whole range of emotions was rushing through her body. How was he going to handle this? How was she? Had they to go on pretending they hadn't met already? It was ludicrous. And wonderful. He must have followed her straightaway. Jumped in the car and followed. But how did he know where she was going?

They shook hands and she didn't want him to let go. But then she thought of Moyra and the strong hand grip faded.

"I didn't know you were home, Shane," said Jane.

"Yes, I've just been abroad. In the Canaries."

"What a coincidence. Isn't it, Lorne?" Jane's keen eyes held hers.

"Yes."

"Why?" asked Shane.

"Well, that's where Lorne lives now. Lanzarote."

"Really?" Shane's eyes were expressionless. "Do you like it?"

"I certainly do. In fact, I can't wait to get back to the island," Lorne replied coolly. She'd regained her poise and was squashing her stupid emotions again. He was *not* going to get the better of her. Play with her this way. And he looked as if he knew it. She picked up her bag. "I have to go now."

"I'm sorry you won't wait to see John."

"Isn't he here?" asked Shane.

"No, he's on his rounds. Did you want to see him? You're not ill?"

"Never been better. I just wanted a few words about the new practice building."

81

"Sorry, but he'll be back soon. Do you want to wait?" Shane shook his head.

"No. I've a lot to do."

"Shane's firm is building us a new surgery, Lorne."

"Lovely," she replied, wondering how she could keep this up without giving the game away. "I really have to go, Jane. Thanks for everything. I *will* write this time."

"Okay."

"Where are you staying?" he asked. He evidently wished to keep up the charade in front of Jane? She moved towards the door with Jane following.

"About an hour's drive from here."

"I see. Well, thanks, Jane, I'll see John later." He was following too. . . Jane was still watching as Lorne and Shane walked together towards the car. Then, with a diplomatic wave, she closed the front door and went inside.

"Did you follow me here?" snapped Lorne.

"What do you think?"

"And how did you get here so quickly? How did you know where I was?"

He had the nerve to grin. "Shall I show you?"

"I don't really want to know."

"Well, why are you asking? Come on, get in." He took the Mercedes' keys out of her hand.

"What are you doing?"

"You'll see. And we'll never get to that meeting if we don't hurry up. Get in. Please." He was opening the passenger door.

At that moment, she saw Jane's lounge curtains move. Her friend was watching. She stood uncertainly. After all, it *was* his car. She sighed and got in.

Lorne was very surprised when Shane reversed the Mercedes. "I thought we were going back to the hotel," she said as he turned left instead of driving back up the hill out of the village.

"We are." He didn't qualify the remark but sat moodily, eyes intent on the winding, narrow lane which led in the direction of the cliffs and beach.

When Shane looked like that, there was no use arguing. She had seen the dark expression too many times before. His hands manipulated the leather-covered wheel expertly. Was he thinking the same as she? About walking down to the beach arm in arm, kissing, like they had done so many times that wonderful wild time when they were lovers.

They would never do it again. Never. To Lorne's horror, she felt her eyelids sting with hot tears. She turned quickly to stare through the window in case he noticed.

"Memory Lane wasn't a success then?" he asked in the most casual manner imaginable.

"On the contrary," retorted Lorne, taking hold of herself. "It certainly convinced me how things can change. And people."

"Life has to go on," he said. They rounded a corner and, below, the beach was opening up before them, long and beautiful. And the straight margin of the horizon was at eye level as Shane swung the car down the steep hill.

"I know," Lorne said. "Why are we going to the beach, Shane?" She couldn't bear it. There were too many memories. It was cruel of him.

"We're not," he said, swinging to the right suddenly on to a rough track which led to the cliff top through a broad, flat, open valley. She gasped.

The black helicopter was just sitting there like an enormous bluebottle. "You came in that?" she asked.

He nodded: "Fraid so. I told you I was in a hurry." So

that was how he knew where she was. He would have seen the car from the air. Of course, he couldn't land too near the village. "And I ran the rest. I took the short cut. In fact, the work-out did me good." She was thinking of him circling over the fields, looking for her, and *running* to find her. Why? Given his earlier behaviour.

"A pity you didn't bring the horse as well," she remarked sarcastically. She couldn't make sense of it all - and she wasn't going to allow herself to hope. It was no use.

He grinned and, for a brief moment, their eyes met familiarly like they'd done on the drive from the airport. But the brief point of contact was gone as he brought the Mercedes to a halt.

"What are you going to do with the car? Just leave it?"

"Someone will be over to pick it up." He took the keys out of the ignition and, opening the door, got out. Next moment, he was coming round to the passenger side.

As she got out of the car, she was almost in his arms but, then, he was drawing back. "Come on," he added, taking her arm. Leaving the Mercedes, Shane and Lorne hurried over to the helicopter, the sea wind blowing hard in their faces. Next moment, he was helping her on board.

* * *

If Lorne hadn't been feeling so strung-up, she would have thrilled to the thought of flying side by side with Shane over the beautiful Cornish landscape. He was as good a pilot as he was everything else.

She had the opportunity to study his profile as his eyes were intent on the instruments. Not classic, but ruggedly handsome. She watched his sure hands, switching instruments on and off; hands which had given her so much pleasure.

There was a tiny throb inside her as she thought of that wonderful night in Lanzarote, but she turned her mind away purposefully at the painful memory. Did nothing last with him? Move him? What about Moyra?

But, again, her heart was battling it out with her sense as it told her how good their loving had been - that the brief interlude must have meant something; that he wouldn't have come chasing after her if it didn't . . .

And all he and she were talking about was mundane and technical with Shane pointing out the landmarks below as if she was a stranger.

Lorne's heart was thumping when she thought of all the personal questions she really wanted to ask him. But now wasn't the time. And that's just what they needed. Time. To sort things out. To tell each other the truth.

At least, if they'd been driving in the Mercedes it might have been easier but, suddenly, Lorne was wearily thankful they were up there in the sky, its vast blueness a wheeling, vacant space above her head.

Below, the jigsaw green of the landscape and the grey-blue of the sea unrolled as Shane flew the company helicopter steadily back across the map that was beautiful North Cornwall.

* * *

CHAPTER 6

Lorne was even wearier when the day was over. The meeting had gone well although she had had nothing to do with it. She hadn't even taken a conscious part. Rather she had let the discussions just wash over her.

Lance had been waiting at the complex's helipad when they'd landed, his hair and suit flapping in the strong wind the rotors made. Lorne was feeling withdrawn and strained when she got down. It was the first thing he'd commented on:

"You don't look too good, honey. Chopper sick?" Trust Lance to make her feel worse. And Shane was taking her arm.

"Come on, Lorne, let's get you in. The sooner the meeting's over, the sooner you can have a rest." She was surprised by the words. Perhaps Shane really did care how she felt? But, no, otherwise he would have said something meaningful to her by now.

They'd hurried into the complex and the wind-blown Lorne was mightily thankful just to get to her room, shower and change.

She was far too busy after that to think of her relationship with Shane, although as she and Lance sat in the board room with him and two of his directors, she found she was having to discipline herself to concentrate on the business in hand and nothing personal at all. And she didn't succeed.

But when she finally got to bed that night, she couldn't sleep. She was too confused and hurt. . . They'd taken an early dinner and she had been forced to watch Moyra enjoying herself with both her conquests.

Certainly, Lance had been added to the list. Lorne wasn't sure what her boss's game was, but he appeared to be playing it very successfully, flirting with Moyra, while she played up to him, laughing at even the weakest of his jokes.

Shane's response to Moyra and Lance's behaviour was an aloofness which, as dinner progressed, grew into icy silence. But Lance appeared to be too thick-skinned to notice and Moyra completely ignored the evident atmosphere.

As Lance drooled over the former, Lorne was ready to believe Shane didn't care for Moyra after all. But they were together, weren't they? But it was evident that it was no longer a happy nor even viable relationship? So why was it continuing?

And Lorne's position was worst of all. All evening, she had watched the trio - Moyra, Shane and Lance playing with her emotions and theirs - as if she was an outsider in some awful nightmare.

She couldn't have lived like that with anyone. Just what was Shane up to? Had he changed so much? Become so heartless? She just didn't understand. And how could he have made love to her? *And how could Lorne have let him?*

She left the table about nine-thirty, saying she had a headache. By the look on Lance's face, he was glad to get rid of her. Moyra, too. And Shane? How would she ever know what he was thinking? Whether he cared?

87

Later, in the claustrophobic privacy of the hotel bedroom, her memory just seemed to centre on that past awful encounter with Moyra Trevise the night Lorne had packed her suitcases and left Westonman village for what she believed would be for ever.

But she'd returned. The sickening memories hit her again and again like slaps in the face and twisted themselves into her heart like daggers.

That terrible time Lorne would never forget because a moment in her life, which should have been utterly beautiful, had been reduced to sadness and despair . . .

* * *

John had confirmed it. Lorne had signed up as his patient when she had first come to Westonman and she was glad it was him, not her family doctor at home, who had broken the news. She had got up off the bed feeling apprehensive and come round the screen.

"Sit down, Lorne," he'd said. Jane's husband was kind; a doctor you could have faith in. He leaned back in the chair.

"Well?" Lorne had noticed how white her knuckles were as she held on to the edge of his desk.

"Yes. It's as you suspected. You're three months pregnant." John's wise eyes held hers for a sympathetic moment, then flicked over to the computer screen in front of him. "I'll be able to give you something for the sickness. It won't harm the baby. But I'd like you to get booked into the hospital with the consultant."

As he scrolled through the drug data on the VDU, he didn't ask her who the father was. But Lorne knew he'd guessed. As John kept on talking, Lorne's mind was drifting from one thing to another.

She wasn't sorry. How could she be with Shane's baby growing inside her? She loved him more than anything or anyone in the world. And he'd be happy about it. She knew he would.

They'd talked of a future together anyway. She had to admit it had been unwise to get herself in the situation. She should have known better but they'd been carried away. Things between them were totally intense.

For instance, that wonderful time on the cold, deserted beach where they were mad enough not to bother about the wind nor the angry sea throwing itself against the rocks. Instead, the sound of the waves had seemed to urge them on and make their passion stronger . . .

Lorne knew that's when it had happened. And the thought of having Shane's baby was wonderful and awful all together. She was so confused the day John confirmed it, she couldn't think of anything except finding Shane and telling him; letting him share the responsibility of that magic moment. But he was away on business.

"What are you going to do, Lorne?" Jane had said.

"What do you mean *do*?" asked Lorne. Jane's eyes were searching her face.

"I mean are you going to have it?"

"Of course I'm going to have it? Shane and I have talked about our future. He'll be over the moon. I know he will."

"Well, that's wonderful," replied Jane, hugging her. As the practice nurse, she'd been with John when he'd examined Lorne and had been waiting to see her when she'd emerged from the surgery. "When are you going to tell him?"

"I can't. He's away," said Lorne. "Funny isn't it? I feel all churned up inside. You know the ones I'm really afraid of telling are my parents. And the headmistress."

"I know. It's understandable. Now, you look really pale.

I think you should go up to the flat and I'll make you a nice cup of tea."

"Tea? No, I don't think so." Lorne had quite gone off it. "What about some of that peach-flavoured lemonade of yours?" Jane had grinned knowingly.

"I see, fads already. Okay, coming up." They'd embraced again and Lorne had hurried upstairs, her heart beating fast with excitement and hope. But the feeling didn't last.

About an hour later, Lorne had woken from an uneasy sleep to answer a knock on her door. Jane was standing there with a worried look in her eyes.

"Is something the matter?" Lorne had said. It was then she learned that there was someone downstairs asking to see her urgently. To her horror, a few moments later, Jane was showing Moyra Trevise into her flat and closing the door behind her. Lorne would never, never forget that awful conversation . . .

Moyra had sat opposite her in the comfortable armchair Lorne had bought from Ikea. She was dressed expensively as usual. In fact, even the most casual clothes - on that day, Levis and cream sweater - made Moyra look a million dollars. She had a broad Alice band holding back her luxuriant dark hair and her eyebrows were arched in perfect half moons as she looked at Lorne.

"I think we should talk," had been her opening gambit. If only Lorne had known the following moves of this very dangerous game.

"Really?" said Lorne, who was feeling extremely sick physically but stronger otherwise. If Moyra had come to talk about herself and Shane, well, surely, Lorne had the best hand. After all, she was carrying his child even though she hadn't told him yet. "Let's do that." She sat back and crossed her legs but, inside, she was trembling, forcing herself not to run for the bathroom. It would be so undignified in front of someone like Moyra.

"About Shane," said Moyra deliberately.

"Shane?" Lorne feigned innocence. Moyra was leaning forward and her face was like a beautiful mask. That was the first time that Lorne wondered how on earth Shane could ever love her. She seemed ruthless and calculating.

"Yes." And Moyra certainly didn't believe in holding anything back either. She went straight for the throat. "I don't think you should see him any more."

"You don't think I should see him any more?" repeated Lorne. She couldn't believe the cheek of the girl. "Well, that is a pity."

"Don't fool about with me," snarled Moyra. "At least, I think we should try to be civilised about this."

"Civilised?" asked Lorne incredulously. "You come here and tell me I shouldn't be seeing Shane Westonman. Why shouldn't I? He's single. I am as well. And anyway it isn't your business." Lorne had gone very hot suddenly and hoped she wasn't going to faint.

"It is my business though. Shane and I have an understanding." The fainty feeling was going off and Lorne felt like laughing now at the stupidity of the situation. Since she'd been pregnant, she'd had these quicksilver changes of mood. It was probably her hormones.

"I think you should go," she said.

"I don't think so," retorted Moyra. "We're going to talk this one out."

"Look, this is my flat and I don't want you here. My relationship with Shane is up to me and him. Not you. Now please will you go."

"Sorry. The answer's no." Moyra was glaring straight at her and Lorne was suddenly reminded of a snake's cold stare as it fixed its victim. That was what Moyra was like - some glittering cobra ready to strike.

"Then . . ." Lorne hesitated for a moment, "then . . . I shall call Jane. You'll have to go then. We really have nothing to discuss."

"I see I'm going to have to tell you the truth," said Moyra. Lorne's heart was giving funny little jumps. Tell her what? "I think you'll feel different when you've heard what I have to say." Even her tone was threatening now. Lorne could hear the sharp edge in her voice slicing through the atmosphere between them.

"I doubt it."

"Shane is two-timing you." Lorne's heart lurched suddenly. "You see, you have to listen."

"I don't believe you."

"You are such a naive little fool, Lorne. You can't have him. He's been going out with me for years. He's in love with me. It was just he was lonely while I was away. But now I'm back to stay. He doesn't want you. Really he doesn't."

"How dare you come here and say that. How dare you," flamed Lorne.

"Yes, that's right. Get upset. I would if I were you. In fact, I'd kill him if it was serious with you and him. But he's told me it isn't. When I phoned him last night . . ." Moyra leaned back triumphantly.

"You're lying as well as insulting. You're making all this up because you're jealous. Because you can't bear the thought a girl has come along who can make Shane really happy. Now will you please get out my flat."

"I'm not jealous, Lorne," said Moyra and the smile which was working her curved, carefully-painted lips didn't reach her cold eyes, "I'm pregnant." Moyra's terrible words hit Lorne as hard as if she'd slapped her.

Looking back, Lorne knew that the look on her face must have betrayed how utterly devastated she felt. . .

"Pregnant?" she repeated in the husky whisper which had become her voice.

"Yes, I'm going to have Shane's child - and he asked me to marry him when I told him." Moyra leaned back. "It happened after Christmas. After I came back from Oxford. That's why I gave up the MBA. Of course, we're over the moon about it. . ."

Lorne was trying to collect her thoughts. It had been Christmas when she and Shane had really begun their affair. When she'd been Greensleeves at the school ball. It couldn't be true. Could it? She was screaming out to him from inside her heart. *Don't let it be true, Shane. Please don't let it be true!*

She tried to make one last stand against Moyra. "I can't believe it," she said. "Christmas was when he and I started to go out."

"I know. And he told me why. You see - after he and I were carried away by our feelings - we go back such a long way - in fact we've shared a whole life together - we had a stupid quarrel. Naturally, I love him. And I wanted to get married straightaway, but he said with all the travelling he does at the moment he wouldn't make a very good husband - and, it was stupid, I suppose - but we had a blazing row. You know what he's like. . ."

Lorne couldn't answer. She felt dead inside as Moyra continued, "And, I suppose, he was turning to you for comfort. I'm sorry, really I am, but you can see that with this happening I need him and, anyway, you wouldn't want to go on going out with him knowing this, would you? No woman would, I should think, in full possession of the facts. I know I couldn't bear being treated like that, if I were you."

Lorne watched Moyra picking up her handbag. She still couldn't say a word. Moyra dusted down her immaculate jeans. "It's a pity, Lorne," she said, "having to tell you like this. You look shocked. We want to keep it a secret about the baby as long as possible, at least until we've fixed the date of the wedding.

"You won't mention it, will you? You know, you've gone very pale. Perhaps you should fix yourself a drink? But you're quite nice-looking. I'm sure you'll be able to replace Shane pretty soon." That was the last straw.

Lorne struggled to her feet, trying to salvage at least some little dignity. "Get out!" she said.

Moyra nodded. "Yes, of course, I realise you're cut up about this. It's a bit of a problem with Shane. He has a roving eye, but I expect he'll settle down - what with the baby and everything. I'm sorry but you just don't count. Shane and I were made for each other. If only you hadn't come on the scene, everything would have been all right." Lorne walked over and held open the door, briefly closing her eyes as her rival went through. She had no defence against this. It was a terrible, unbelievable situation. All Lorne could think of in that hopeless moment was *thank God, I haven't told him*.

With the sound of Moyra's heels clattering down the stairs resounding in her ears, Lorne flopped down on the settee and began to cry and laugh hysterically at the same time.

A worried Jane had found her like that and had called John in from the surgery straightaway to take a look at her, but it was at least an hour or so before Lorne was able to tell either of them anything about the dreadful experience she had just been through.

Even then, she couldn't bring herself to tell them Moyra's bombshell about her being pregnant as well. Instead, she told them that Moyra had said Shane had asked her to marry him and she'd accepted . . .

John and Jane couldn't do anything to comfort Lorne, could they? Only give her their support. They went over every eventuality, every suggestion. Telling Shane about Lorne's baby and not telling him; trying to decide if Moyra was lying. In fact, they considered absolutely everything.

But there was no way out. John insisted Shane would want to know about Lorne's baby - after all, he was the father, but Lorne wouldn't hear of it. No way was she going to tell him after Moyra's disclosure. And, besides, could she ever trust him again? Jane had been on Shane's side at first. She didn't like Moyra at all and had said that Lorne should get on to Shane immediately and find out, but Lorne didn't want to hear another word. She even screamed at them both which was quite out of character, saying she wasn't going to trap Shane and put him in an invidious position. Ironic words given Lorne's own.

She had sat for a whole hour on the side of her bed with her hands over her ears, rocking herself to and fro which did her no good at all. And, after, she'd been sick about ten times.

But the worst about the whole thing was she still loved Shane. And, silly though it was, whatever he was really like, two-timer or not; whatever he had done, she would always love him, body and soul. It was the most awful dilemma any girl ever had to face, but when she came back to herself she knew she certainly wasn't the first to end up that way, nor would she be the last.

And Lorne *had* faced it. It had been a very sad time when she left Westonman village for what she believed was for ever. Jane had seen her off on the train, her kind eyes full of tears.

"I wish it had been different, Lorne," she'd said. "Do you think you've made the right decision?"

"How could I tell him, Jane? How could I? It was my

fault for being so stupid. I shouldn't have fallen like that. I should have taken precautions but I suppose I thought he loved me and we were going to be together forever but - don't let's go over it all again. I'll be fine, really I will. Dad and Mum have been smashing about it. I'll be okay at home. And so will the baby . . ." But none of it had been all right. . .

* * *

Lorne went over that awful time hundreds of times afterwards and, lying in her lonely hotel bedroom, she couldn't help thinking about that lost baby of hers and Shane's. Of course, all the worry had brought on the birth prematurely and there'd been no hope of it surviving. It had been a little boy.

And she knew in her heart that her parents had felt it had all turned out for the best. It had taken a very long time to get over the whole traumatic experience and, finally, she had taken that job with Lance in the Canaries. They'd been in total agreement with that as well.

Lorne had travelled a very long way from London and Cornwall to forget. *Until Shane Westonman had come back into her life again. To make her suffer again. But where was that child of his and Moyra's? And the wedding Moyra had talked about?* Nothing added up. Neither Shane's current behaviour to her or with Moyra Trevise. Lorne just had to find out the truth about what made him really tick.

Suddenly she couldn't control herself. She was angry with herself for crying but she couldn't help it. But just as Lorne was scrubbing the tears away with a tissue, she heard someone knocking. She lay still, hoping whoever it was would go away. She didn't want to see anyone. But the noise was insistent.

Finally, pulling on her robe, she went up to the door and stood uncertainly, "Who is it?"

"Lance." She looked at her watch.

"What time do you call this? You've woken me up," she called irritably.

"It's only midnight. I need to talk."

"Won't it do in the morning?" She leaned her forehead against the door. He was the last one she wanted to talk to.

"No."

"All right," she sighed. After all, he was the boss. She turned the knob and opened the door. She could see something had upset him the moment she let him in. He was wearing only his dressing gown. Lance strode across the room and flung himself down on the couch. Next moment he said:

"Have you anything to drink?"

"I don't know."

"Well, look in the ice box, will you?"

She ignored his tone. She was used to Lance. His manners were always abominable when anything upset him. "Okay." A moment later, she was standing in the suite's small kitchen surveying the contents of the refrigerator. "Whisky? Beer?" There was everything. "Double Scotch." She found a glass and, after pouring him a big one, carried it out.

"Aren't you having one?" he said, as she handed it to him.

"No, I don't want to make my headache any worse."

"You've been crying," he accused.

"I haven't."

"Your nose is all red," he retorted, throwing the spirit down his throat. "That's better." He closed his eyes briefly.

"You shouldn't drink when you're upset. It's a bad

habit," said Lorne. She could be just as irritable when she wanted to. "Anyway, what do you want to talk about? I'm tired."

"I don't like being set-up," he said.

"How have you been *set-up*?"

"Westonman. And that girl friend of his. She's a little cow."

"You didn't seem to think so earlier on," reminded Lorne sarcastically.

"Maybe I didn't. But I know better now."

"In other words," said Lorne, sitting down as far away as she could, "she gave you the brush-off."

Lance's green eyes were just slits. "I don't take that from anyone," he snarled.

"Come on, Lance, I know you," Lorne snapped back.

"Yeah, I suppose you do," said Lance, strafing her body with his eyes. "When the heck will I ever understand women? She gave me the come-on."

"Never mind Moyra, what's Shane done?"

"He's an arrogant bastard. He's pulled the plug on the project. He won't give an inch."

"I imagine he wasn't too keen on you making up to Moyra," said Lorne.

"That I can't believe," said Lance. "She more or less told me she didn't care a toss about him. *Stupid bitch.*"

Lorne's heart lurched.

"Well, what else has happened?"

"I'm evidently not a big enough fish for Westonman to fry," answered Lance bitterly. "Seems he's decided to change direction. Down under. He's just told me."

"What?"

"Aussieland. Northern Territories. He's flying out next week."

"Well, why do you think he invited us over here in the

98

first place?" Lorne's brain was telling her to be careful and not let Lance know a thing about her and Shane, but her heart was screaming out that Shane was going away and she might never see him again.

"Search me? The man's a bloody sadist," quipped Lance, making for the kitchen. He returned with a refill.

"Well, it won't do you any good to get drunk," said Lorne.

"I know, but I feel like it. Anyway, we've our own backers on the island. They won't let me down. We're going tomorrow." Lorne realised that Lance's mood stemmed from sheer disappointment. He had ambition. And he liked running with the big boys. It served him right. He was so cocky. But he was still her employer.

"That's okay then. Now you've told me, I think you should get off to bed."

"Sure." His eyes swivelled towards the bedroom.

"No, Lance, not here. *Your* bed," said Lorne. She walked over to the door and opened it.

"You're heartless, honey, you know that?" He was unsteady on his feet already.

"No, just sensible."

"You think it might be different back home?"

"I doubt it," she said. "Even if you're sober."

"I never am when I'm near you," he retorted. Next moment, he had his arms fast round her. His breath smelled of the whisky and his eyes were very bright.

"Let me go, Lance," she said, trying to struggle free.

"Not likely," he said and, next moment, he'd bent her backwards in the doorway and clamped his wet mouth over hers. Lorne, gasping with surprise, was trying to pull her robe closed when, at that very moment, a loud voice said:

"Goodnight." Lance jumped and let Lorne go and, as the two of them broke apart, they saw Shane. He was still wearing black tie and his dark, hard eyes reflected his sober attire as did the serious look on his face.

"Don't let me interrupt you," he said coolly and walked swiftly past, away and round the corner of the hotel corridor.

Lorne gritted her teeth and, with all her might, pushed the unsteady Lance out over the threshold and slammed her door to.

Then she ran across the suite into the bedroom and, flung herself on the bed angrily. Next moment, she was hammering the pillow with her fists, tears of frustration and disappointment running down her cheeks. . .

* * *

Lorne had discarded the ice-pink blouse and soft colours she'd arrived in, for navy business attire. It suited her mood.

She glanced at her watch as she waited for the car to arrive to take them back to the airport. Shane wouldn't be driving them back. And, thank God, there'd be no Moyra either.

She looked across at her boss. Lance was taking a call on his mobile phone and she hoped he wouldn't be on long. All she wanted was to get away from the hotel and Cornwall.

She walked across Reception, over to the huge windows and stared out miserably. It had been a mistake to come here as she thought it would. She should have stuck out for staying behind - and then none of this would have happened. The memories had been getting dimmer.

Coming here with Lance had dragged everything to the surface. All that old baggage she was carrying inside herself. All that pain. She felt raw and terribly vulnerable. But she still cared about Shane.

Lorne concluded there had to be something the matter with her. When Shane had seen her and Lance together last night she should have been glad to let him think they were lovers. It would have paid him out. The way he had treated her had been abominable. Leading her on again. After all he'd done to her.

Lorne felt quite desperate about everything as she looked out at the wonderful landscape Shane had created. His own bit of Paradise. It was horrible.

She could have run screaming across the beautiful parkland below and flung herself off the top of the cliffs. Instead, her anger was bottled up inside and festering. She turned away from the window, telling herself off for even thinking that way. She had to be positive. She sauntered back across the reception area. Lance was still on the phone, huddled by the entrance to the fitness club. Lorne sighed and sat down. Instead of looking at a magazine, she leaned her head against the back of the luxurious chair and closed her eyes.

"Lorne." She jumped. Looked up. Shane was standing over her. "You okay?"

"Perfectly," she replied, knowing her lips were set in a thin, defiant line. "Why shouldn't I be?"

"You look tired."

"I am." Her tone was brittle too.

He was wearing a sober pin-striped suit, looked the epitome of every corporate business man, but her heart still fluttered whenever he was near. It probably would forever. Lorne told herself off again for being so hopelessly charmed by Shane.

"I'm sorry. Perhaps you'll get a rest on the plane."

"Perhaps. But I doubt it."

"You and Lance have a lot to discuss." Inside, she felt angry at the brief inference. He thought she and

101

Lance were together. It made her sick. He should have known.

"Yes. Naturally we're disappointed things didn't turn out."

"So am I." His enigmatic dark eyes probed her face. It was no good pretending he was sorry. Shane was an arrogant bastard.

Suddenly, Lorne wanted to scream at him, batter her fists against his chest, shout, *Why the hell did you bring me here? Why did you make love to me? Make me want you again?* But all she gave was a brief nod. They were like strangers.

"The car's here," he added.

"Lance is on the phone." Shane's eyes flicked in his direction.

"Are you happy - working with him?"

"Yes," she lied. "I'm doing what I like. Why?"

"Just wondered." Small talk was ridiculous at a time like this. They might never see each other again. Lorne's heart lurched. But wasn't that what she wanted? And him as well?

Suddenly, Lance was off and coming over. Shane held out his hand. The American and he shook hands briefly.

"Sorry it didn't work out, Denver."

"So am I. But it's not a disaster. We're big enough to take it." Lance grinned but the smile didn't reach those narrow, green eyes. Lorne knew him well enough to know he was cursing Shane inside.

"Your car's here. Well, thanks for coming. We'll keep in touch?"

"Perhaps. And thanks for a great couple of days. Lorne?" Lance was turning for the door.

"Thank you, Shane," she said and her voice seemed far away and icy-cold.

Next moment, she felt his warm breath as he kissed her briefly on the cheek. Being in his arms even for that short time made her tremble. She withdrew not trusting herself to reply. She nodded and hurried off behind Lance out of the hotel.

As the chauffeur opened the door of the Rolls, Lorne glimpsed back. Shane was standing alone at the top of the hotel steps, a tall, black figure. Then, he turned abruptly and was swallowed up inside.

Lance had been watching him too. He gave a brief nod, "And good riddance, I say." He settled himself comfortably against the luxurious leather. "The guy's a kook, bringing us over here for nothing. I tell you, Lorne," he breathed, squeezing her elbow, "when we get on his jet we'll crack open a couple of bottles of his best champagne. He owes us one. Him and that broad. By the way, sorry about last night. I was out of order. Frustration, I guess. But, I tell you what, he'll be sorry. He's missing out on a great deal."

As the car rolled round the corner where Lorne had almost collided with Shane on his horse, she rummaged in her bag for her handkerchief and, staring miserably at nothing through the car window, blew her nose fiercely.

* * *

CHAPTER 7

Lorne just couldn't stop worrying about it. She couldn't concentrate on anything. It seemed like Morton's excited voice was coming from miles away.

Lance's son kept on pestering her to bury him in the sand, "Come on, Lorne, come on. Please." But Lorne felt far too lazy to do anything. In fact, she couldn't care less.

It wasn't like her to be like this for weeks. But she'd been the same ever since she'd returned from Cornwall. She was so on edge - and she felt unwell. Whatever was the matter with her? Lorne couldn't bear even to admit to herself what she was worried about. It was like history repeating itself. But she'd soon be sure . . .

"Lorne, what's the matter? You're not looking."

"Morton, you're a pest. Can't you see I'm having a rest." Next moment, a small, brown hand was planted firmly on her midriff. "Get off, you're making me all sandy," she snapped, pushing the tickling fingers away.

"Gee, you are stressed out," persisted Lance's precocious son, his green eyes dancing with mischief.

"No, I'm not. Your Dad's been working me hard. I'm relaxing. Go plague your granny!" Morton sighed,

"Okay. But you're not half as much fun as you used to be." His aggrieved tone was so much like Lance's, it startled Lorne. She shook her head at him and the sand from her body. Next moment, the little boy was running off to where Lilly Denver was sitting under a multi-coloured umbrella.

The elderly lady caught Lorne's eye and grimaced. Yes, Morton was a handful. And, suddenly, Lorne was back to square one. Where she'd been before Shane Westonman's letter had upset her world.

It would be so easy to give in to Lance. To fall under Morton's toothy spell. They'd make a nice little family. And Lilly would love to have her as part of it. Lance was on the golf course and the three of them were spending their usual time together on the beach. Yes, her life could be rosy - if Lorne agreed. *But she didn't want Lance.* Shane Westonman and Cornwall were still holding on fast to her heart and, once again, she was being an utter, utter fool. Especially now.

Glancing across, she watched Morton, a tin of Coke in his hand, engrossed completely in something Lilly was showing him. The little boy didn't have a care in the world. Sighing, Lorne tried to relax but, whenever she thought of her afternoon appointment, her stomach turned over. . .

* * *

Dr Tomas Garcia was tapping the end of his pen lightly on the table as Lorne came out of the cubicle. Then he nodded to the nurse who, with a brief smile, slipped tactfully out of the door.

"Come and sit down, Lorne." His dark eyes smiled sympathetically out of a smooth, olive-skinned face. "How are you feeling?"

"I'll tell you in a minute. Well, doctor?"

"Yes, you were right. You're pregnant."

Lorne closed her eyes briefly and swallowed. She must be the unluckiest girl alive. Once, she'd thought herself the luckiest. She opened them and looked straight at the Spanish doctor. *How could she have fallen again?* She damn well knew *how* but it didn't make her feel any better. What a bloody awful mess. *But she had to face it. She was pregnant by Shane. What was she going to do?*

Dr Tomas must have noticed the stricken look but he was too professional to make a comment. He nodded slightly and, naturally, was again far too professional to ask who was the father. That would be unethical.

"I shall be very happy to look after you, Lorne, so please don't worry. The nurse will provide you with some information leaflets - and you'll have to come to the surgery for regular checks. And, of course, you will need to see a consultant especially as it's your first." He smiled, scrutinising her face.

Lorne's heart was thumping. She knew she was going to have to tell him. But perhaps he could tell already?

"Now I suggest you go home and have a rest. But, before you do, I'll just check your blood pressure. You're looking tired."

Lorne sat, eyes fixed on the desk as the rubber apparatus constricted her arm. After a few seconds, Dr Garcia stopped pumping and listened carefully. Then he took the stethoscope out of his ears.

"Absolutely fine," he smiled. "You're very fit, Lorne. Not sick, I hope."

"Not at the moment. Just queasy."

"Good. Well, I suggest you keep on taking care of yourself. Any other problems?"

"Just one, doctor," said Lorne, swallowing. She hesitated. "I've been pregnant before. And I lost the baby." She stared Garcia straight in the eyes.

106

Dr Tomas took in the information quickly. He'd always admired Lorne for her beauty and her brains. And for her English reserve, which was in short supply in most of the Spanish resorts.

He admitted to liking Lorne very much. And he could see by her face she had been unhappy in the past and that this news wasn't making her much happier. He wondered then who the father was. Probably Denver. But, as a doctor, he was constantly surprised by his patients.

"I see," he said, tapping his pencil on her notes. "Well, that does make a difference. Perhaps you'd better fill me in on your past history then." Dr Garcia leaned back, his kindly face impassive.

Breathing in deeply, Lorne sat back too and began to tell him the story of her miscarriage in London. It was very painful indeed. . .

* * *

As she was walking out of the hall leading from Dr Garcia's surgery, Lorne caught a glimpse of herself in a mirror. She looked as pale and tired as she felt. It had been a real ordeal telling the doctor about her medical history but it had been necessary. Dr Garcia had pointed out to her the need to rest. He hadn't asked any personal questions. He was Lance's doctor as well and she supposed he thought her boss was the father. Tomas and Lance were good friends. They played golf together and Garcia knew how much Lance thought of her.

Lance was always shooting his mouth off about how much they liked each other and, of course, Lorne often accompanied him both at social and business meetings. She also looked after his son.

For that reason, Lorne suddenly decided she was going

to tell Garcia that Lance wasn't the father. She was sure he'd never put his foot in it given medical ethics. But, who knows? She couldn't risk it.

"One thing - I'm sure I don't need to say this but I'm going to."

"Of course."

"Lance is not the father."

The doctor nodded slightly. "You have no need to say anything else, Lorne. If any confidence between doctor and patient was breached, I'd be in serious trouble. Please put it out of your mind." And that was the end of it.

Yes, Dr Garcia had been very serious about her taking it easy. He had pointed out the dangers if she didn't. How was she going to rest without anyone suspecting? First of all, there was her job and, secondly, she was going to have to tell Lance sooner or later. He'd know it wasn't his baby.

There seemed no answer to any of Lorne's problems. If only things had been different between her and Shane, how happy she would have been.

She couldn't bear the thought of it. Once again, Shane had a right to know about the baby but there was no way she felt able to give him such news - not after what had happened.

With exactly the same feelings of desperation she'd experienced before, a pale-faced Lorne walked over to her car and unlocked it. It was stiflingly hot inside and, quickly, she wound down all the windows. The Canarian air was full of blowing sand, which wasn't at all pleasant. Most of the locals, including her, knew better than to be out in it. She was determined to go straight home and rest her aching head.

She wound up the windows again preferring to suffer the heat rather than the sand. All around her, tourists, in beach wear, were jostling each other on the pavements, enjoying themselves. It seemed so unfair. That's what she should have been doing. But it was all her own fault falling for Shane again. Uncharacteristically, tears were coming into her eyes at the thought. She was probably going to become over-emotional from now on.

Breathing in to calm herself, she switched on the ignition. One thing Dr Garcia had *not* suggested was a termination. That would have been unethical seeing Lorne was in excellent health. But there was no way in the world Lorne would ever contemplate aborting Shane's and her baby, even if he had. And she had to take the doctor's advice and look after herself. It was only sensible. She couldn't bear to lose another baby, could she?

Ramming the little Seat into gear, an anxious Lorne drove off into the crazy traffic in the direction of Teguise.

* * *

Lance Denver was sitting behind his mahogany office desk, fiddling with his pen. He was wearing a white linen suit and appeared cool and calm. But Lorne could tell nothing was further from the truth. The way his green eyes had been appraising her body for the last half an hour gave him away. Also he stopped frequently to loosen his tie as if he had something urgent to say.

She was sitting opposite him and intended to keep it that way. Lorne was pretending to concentrate but it was a particularly hot day and she felt nauseated because Lance had insisted on an unusually early start. It had been all she could do to get out of bed. And, of course, she'd had no breakfast. She was hoping sincerely that she wouldn't faint; also that there was no sign yet as to her present condition.

Suddenly, she was forced to lean over and take a sip of water from the cut-glass tumbler in front of her. Then, her hands shaking slightly, she continued to look over the spreadsheet on which the two of them were working.

"I know there's something the matter, Lorne," said Lance. "You can't fool me. You've been like this ever since that damn fool trip to England." Her heart lurched and, for a moment, she went dizzy.

"Is it something I've done?" he continued. He smacked down the pen and gave the chair an impatient half-swivel. "Is it because of my behaviour with that Englishman's girlfriend? The two-timing Moyra. Lorne, it didn't mean a thing. It's always been you from the first moment you came to me for a job."

So she'd been right. She steeled herself for what was coming.

Lance swivelled his chair again and, jumping out of it, stood up and leaned over the desk. "You're going to tell me what's the matter, Lorne. And that's an order."

She was eyeing him warily. There was one thing she couldn't stand at that moment. Having to fight off Lance. But, as usual, he was persistent.

"You haven't been feeling well for ages, Lorne, have you? Even when we went out to dinner with Westonman. That was when it came on, wasn't it? I think you should go see Garcia. I can have a word with him if you like."

"I have been," retorted Lorne. Lance stared in surprise. "And there's absolutely nothing wrong with me. He said so. It's just the heat."

"Well, you never suffered from it before," Lance replied. He had left his chair now and was standing beside her. He put a hand on her shoulder and left it there.

Lorne was very uncomfortable as she experienced the slight pressure. Since she'd found out she was pregnant,

110

she'd felt extremely vulnerable. And she could do without a row with Lance. But it was inevitable. Sooner or later, he was going to notice anyway. And then what would he do?

She pushed back her hair, shaking off his hand. "Now, please, can we get on? Otherwise, I'll never finish this."

"Sure," he replied, patting her shoulder instead. But he made no move to sit down again. She could almost feel his eyes boring into her as she bowed her head over the work. He was ready for one last try.

Next moment, he was lifting her chin with his hand. She trembled in spite of herself with a mixture of anger and desperation.

She shook her head. "Please let's get on, Lance, there's nothing the matter." But he wouldn't have it.

Her aching head heard him ask again, "What's gone wrong between us, Lorne? We used to be close. You know I still care for you. A lot. And so does Morton. The three of us could be very happy." With a swift movement, he was squatting in front of her.

"Please, Lance, please!" she remonstrated, looking at his tanned hand on her knee. "I can't stand this just now."

"Neither can I. For God's sake, Lorne, I'm not asking you to *live* with me. Don't you understand? I'm asking you to be my *wife*. It'd be great for all of us. Me, Morton, Lilly. We all love you, Lorne."

"Get up, Lance. Please. Or I will."

He didn't move, just stared up at her with those sharp, green, pleading eyes. She was totally exasperated at his pure persistence.

"I'm sorry. I can't marry you," she snapped. "Or anyone." Pushing him away, she jumped up and walked over to the window.

Next moment, he had followed her. He took her in his

111

arms and she tried to push him away. But he was holding her tightly.

She struggled. "Let me go, Lance. This is stupid. Why won't you understand. I don't love you."

"I love *you* though. Isn't that enough? You *like* me, don't you?"

"No, it's not enough. If I ever get married, it'll be because I love someone desperately." Lorne broke away from him again. "Please don't say anything else. I'm going home."

She grabbed her bag and her briefcase and faced him, although she felt wobbly. "Don't come after me. I mean it. Goodbye, Lance."

It was the first time Lorne had ever walked out on her boss completely and, as she hurried through the door, she found herself wishing that she would never have to put up with Lance Denver's outrageous behaviour again...

* * *

Lilly Denver called two days after Lorne had seen Dr Garcia. She was a direct American lady, not at all like her son, Lance, except for an identical pair of green eyes which, in her case, were not startling nor piercing, just sympathetic.

Lilly thought a lot of Lorne and had said so many times. They had become good friends and, if Lorne had anything against Lance, it didn't extend to his mother. In fact, Lorne had confided in Lilly so many times. If only she could now. Lorne knew that Lilly had been wishing for ages that she and Lance would get together. Lorne remembered her hinting, "What my Lance wants is a good girl to settle him down. The boy's been right out of order ever since his wife left him." But how could she tell Lilly what was really the matter? It would be far too painful.

112

Lorne motioned her to come in and the plump, middle-aged lady, in polka-dotted navy cotton, stepped into the small hall of the flat.

"Please come through, Lilly," said Lorne, "I'm afraid I'm not very tidy."

"I've come to see *you*, not the flat," smiled Lilly, following her inside.

Lorne knew she didn't look her best; she'd just been feeling extremely sick and wondering what she could do about it. She was also wearing old denim shorts and a skimpy top she wouldn't have been seen out in. Her blonde hair was tied back in a ponytail. In fact, she didn't look like the usually glamorous and business-like Lorne at all. She'd telephoned into the office the day after Lance had proposed and said she was going to take a couple of days off. She did have annual leave to come and felt she needed it so she could sort out her own feelings rather than anyone else's.

She turned to Lilly. "Would you like coffee? Iced?"

"No, thank you, dear, I'm watching my caffeine intake."

"I have de-caff," replied Lorne.

Lilly shook her head, her eyes taking in the array of spread-out magazines on the couch and the remains of Lorne's uneaten breakfast on the coffee table.

"As I said I'm in a bit of a mess. I slept in. Do sit down here. It's a very comfortable chair. I often sit in this corner and take in the view."

She led Lilly over to her favourite white chair, which looked out over her bougainvillea-covered balcony.

"Okay?"

Lilly nodded and smiled as she settled herself, fiddling with her handbag as she placed it on the wrought-iron table. She certainly seemed uneasy and Lorne was positive she knew why. Probably Lance had chosen his mother as messenger, sent her to try and break down Lorne's resolve. But Lilly was her friend. She'd understand.

"Is something wrong?" she asked the older woman, mentally preparing herself for what was coming. But it would take more than Lilly Denver to make Lorne change her mind.

"Not with me, dear," replied Lilly, looking keenly at Lorne. "But I wonder what's happening with you. Lance tells me you and he had a fight. And that you're not well. That worries me, you know." Lorne was grateful she'd got to the point straightaway.

"Hardly a fight," she replied. "More like a disagreement, Lilly. And I'm okay healthwise. Really." She breathed in deeply. How much had Lance told his mother? She decided she was going to fetch it out into the open anyway.

"Well, I'm glad to hear it. But what about this fight? What was it for? It's upset Lance a heap. And you don't look too good either. You can call me a nosy old woman but, honestly, I'm worried about you both. Lance thinks so much of you. You know that."

"Yes, I do. And I like working for him." Lorne hesitated, biting her lip.

"Well, then . . ." She could see Lilly didn't understand; could almost taste the atmosphere as a puzzled Lilly waited for the explanation. She was going to *have* to tell her. "You see, Lilly, Lance asked me to marry him yesterday." Lorne could see by her expression that Lilly hadn't expected the news.

"Oh, my dear, I'm so pleased." Lilly went to embrace her, but Lorne moved back

"I said *no*, Lilly." The older woman's eyes flicked wide with surprise and disappointment..

"But, why? You're perfectly suited. And I know you were very close some months ago. What's gone

114

wrong? Forgive me for prying but, perhaps you'll change your mind?"

"No, Lilly, I can't. You see," she paused, swallowing to try and release the awful dry feeling in her mouth, "although I didn't tell Lance, I'm in love with someone else." She was looking directly into Lilly's eyes. It was true. Whatever Shane had done, Lorne was in love with him. *And she would be - forever.*

Lance's mother was shaking her head slightly, as if she couldn't believe what Lorne had said. Next moment, she was asking, "Do I know the guy?" She was also rummaging in her bag for a tissue. She found one and dabbed her eyes. Lorne felt wretched for hurting her. For the umpteenth time she wondered how Lance could have such a very nice mother and have turned out the way he had.

"No, it's someone I met a long time ago in England. And who's turned up again." She heard her words coming from a distance, as if they didn't belong to her. "I thought I was over him. That's why I came out here. But I wasn't."

All perfectly true.

Lorne sat down on the couch gladly, feeling exceedingly queasy, hoping she wasn't going to faint. Lilly was staring out at the view. Lorne knew she was trying to get her feelings under control.

Lorne closed her eyes momentarily and waited. Next moment, Lilly was saying, "Forgive me, Lorne, but, whoever it is, he doesn't seem to be making you very happy." Blunt, but true as well. Lorne was *extremely* unhappy, but could she ever tell Lilly the real reason? She looked across at the older woman.

"I know, but things will change. We'll sort it out." Although it wasn't the truth, just saying it made her feel better.

"And you haven't told my son about this other boy?" Lorne shook her head, horrified to feel tears pricking her eyes. She couldn't cry in front of Lilly. Next moment, Lance's mother was coming over. She sat down on the couch beside Lorne and put her hand on her arm.

"Well, I can't say this was what I wanted to hear but it would be no good between you and Lance if you love someone else, would it? It'd be like him and his wife all over again. I'm afraid my son's unlucky with women. Always getting the wrong idea. Well, well," she sighed, "I really didn't expect to hear this. But there you are, life's never simple, is it?" Her lips were set unsmiling.

"I'm sorry, Lilly, and it was wrong for me to encourage Lance when I first started working for him but I thought I was over this guy. I did try and tell him lots of times." That was true too, but Lance would never take no for an answer.

"He can be a very selfish boy sometimes and I suppose I'm to blame for that, my dear," replied Lilly. "I spoiled him, I suppose, after his father died. But he's been everything to me. And I wanted him to be happy so much." She sniffed.

Next moment, she was reaching into her bag. Lorne watched in horror as Lilly found another tissue and began to dab at the tears which came trickling down her cheeks.

"Please don't cry, Lilly. And it's not true that Lance is selfish." Lorne tried desperately to cheer her up. "And, if he was, it wouldn't be your fault. You've been a wonderful mother to him. Why, Lance relies on you completely. And what would Morton do without you?" Lilly sniffed for a while then, finally, put away her handkerchief. She looked at Lorne and then away, her fingers clutching at her bag.

"Poor Morton. He loves *you* a whole lot too, Lorne. But,

116

never mind. And I won't ask you any more questions."
She sniffed again. "I just hope this guy is worthy of you,
dear. And that *things* get sorted quickly." Lilly Denver
was composing herself now. She looked across at the
kitchen. "I think I could do with that coffee right now."

"Okay," replied Lorne, relieved. "I'll go and put the kettle
on. . .

She stood in the kitchen and leaned on the ice box
door, pressing her burning forehead against its white
coolness. Her stomach was lurching dangerously. She
hoped she wasn't going to be sick.

As the kettle boiled, the nausea receded and she was
feeling almost herself again when she entered the living
room with the tray.

Lilly was standing on the verandah, looking out to
sea. "It's a wonderful view," she said, without looking
round. The brightly-coloured wind-surfers were still
wrestling with the hot wind and the waves and, up in
the bluest of skies, the sun shone on mercilessly.

"Isn't it? I never tire of looking," replied Lorne, putting
down the tray and pouring a cup of coffee. "Sugar?"

Lilly came over to help.

As Lorne handed her the cup, the older woman looked
her straight in the eyes. "I think one of us is going to
have to tell Lance the truth, you know."

"Yes," replied Lorne quickly. "*I* will as soon as I'm ready.
Just give me time. That's why I'm taking a few days off.
To think about it." She put a hand to her head, noticing
suddenly that the room was beginning to whirl. . .

"Good." Lilly was sipping her coffee, looking out to sea
across the verandah. Without glancing at Lorne, she
added, "I wonder when Lance will start teaching Morton
to boardsail? I think it's about time he stopped playing so
much golf and started concentrating on his son.

"I believe children are the most important things in this whole world, my dear, don't you? A child is a God-given gift. When you got 'em, you just have to look after them." Lorne nodded in reply. She couldn't trust herself to say a word. She was feeling extremely strange. . .

A moment later, Lilly Denver was staring as Lorne held on to a piece of furniture to save herself from collapsing.

"I'm sorry, Lilly . . ." she began and then Lance's mother took command and supporting Lorne to the couch, made her sit down and pushed her head between her knees.

When Lorne came up, finally, white and trembling, Lilly's expression was full of sympathetic questions. "I'm sorry. It was foolish of me. I just felt faint. It's the heat"

"Lorne," said the older woman, "I'm old enough to be your ma and I think we've known each other long enough not to be keeping secrets. I know there's something you're not telling me. Forgive me but - this fainting and being sick - are you pregnant?"

Lorne breathed in, then sighed. Lilly was holding her arm firmly. After what seemed like hours, she nodded miserably.

"I take it that the baby isn't Lance's?" Lorne nodded again. "This other boy's?"

"Yes," replied Lorne quietly. . .

A moment later, Lily was stroking back Lorne's hair from her forehead. Lorne just let her. . .

"Well, I guess both of us have some explaining to do. But, honey, you look just awful. I think you'd better start taking care of yourself or Heaven knows what's going to happen to you."

Lorne couldn't trust herself to speak as Lilly lifted her legs on to the couch, looked at the coffee pot, then back at her. "It might be de-caff but I'd prefer to see you drinking something else. Is there any spare milk in the ice box?"

"No need to fuss, Lilly."

"By the look of you, I think there is. No, don't move, I'll get it." Lilly was making for the kitchen when she stopped. "And don't get worrying that I'll let on to that boy of mine. That'll be up to you but I tell you, Lorne, you need to look after number one now."

"Yes, Lilly," replied Lorne, gratefully closing her eyes. At that moment, she felt so rotten she wouldn't have cared if the whole world knew she was pregnant.

* * *

Two days after Lilly's visit, Lorne was staring at the computer screen in the office. She'd decided she felt better at work rather than at home moping round the flat, but her mind was so confused that she couldn't concentrate on much. Lilly had kept her word and mustn't have said anything, because Lance was his usual annoying self. He hadn't tried it on again though. She hoped he'd given up but, sooner or later, she was going to have to tell him the truth. It was then Lorne realised what she'd just read as she was checking the e-mail. The letters on the screen jigged up and down in front of her eyes and she wiped the perspiration from her forehead. She re-read the message. She couldn't believe it. This was all she needed.

Tossing back a strand of damp, blonde hair from her forehead, she glanced quickly at Lance, who never missed a trick. He was staring at her from his seat behind the desk.

"You don't look too great again, honey. Want some fresh air? This air conditioning is crap," he barked.

She could do without Lance's concern at that moment. As he jumped up, she replied, "No, please, don't open the window. There's too much sand in the wind." Lorne gasped,

119

"I'm absolutely fine," as a tiny pain stabbed her stomach.

"Any post?"

"Yes." She leaned back, the cushioned seat of her swivel chair the only thing that was keeping her upright. She felt just as she had done when Lance had first shown her the letter from Shane. She closed her eyes briefly, then opened them to find herself staring into Lance's green ones.

"Take a look," she said, rolling back the chair.

"Well, I'll be damned." Lance was grinning as if he'd won the lottery. "Look at that. Westonman. *Circumstances have changed* have they? *Room for discussion*, eh? So he's ready to eat humble pie?"

"I doubt it," replied Lorne. Her heart was thudding and she really felt quite unwell. For the second time that morning, she hoped she wasn't going to be sick. Lance was rubbing his hands together now. She was thankful that he seemed to have forgotten the state of her health; she knew he was already imagining the size of the deal which Westonman Associates were going to sign with him.

"I knew he'd come round." Lorne could hear Lance's voice from a distance. "These guys are all the same. When they see real money, they just go for it. Well, two can play that game and Denver Inc doesn't come cheap . . ."

"Excuse me a moment." Lorne made a hasty exit, not even hearing his answer.. A few seconds later, as she gripped the small washbasin with clenched white knuckles, all she could do was swear at him inside. For the thought of Shane back on the island was both the worst and the best news she could have ever imagined since the two of them had been part of that painful trip to England.

* * *

CHAPTER 8

Lorne made her way down the white stone steps to the shore. Days after, she remembered particularly noticing how the sea looked; a wonderful inky blue topped with froth. She used to think it was exciting that somewhere over the horizon was the coast of Africa. Today, there was nothing on her mind except the thought that she might bump into Shane on the brief weekend visit he'd arranged with Lance.

It was what she wanted, but she couldn't bear it. Perhaps she ought to tell Shane about the baby? Perhaps he would want to know? But what if Lance wanted them all to go to dinner again. It would be too awful. She just couldn't.

Lorne gritted her teeth. Of course, Shane thought she and Lance were lovers. She remembered the expression on his face when he'd seen them together. And all Lorne had been doing was fighting Lance off. It was so unfair. How had she got herself into such a mess?

"Phew." She wiped the perspiration off her face then, stepping down carefully on to the beach, she waved absent-mindedly to Lilly and Morton, who were in their usual place, protected from the sun by the gaily-coloured umbrellas with the Denver logo. They were beckoning her to come on down.

But all she was thinking of just then was a baby was

the last thing Shane wanted to hear about. It would certainly mess up his life with Moyra. *If he had one*.

Lorne remembered her conversation with Jane. What had her friend said? *They don't get on*. Then why the hell had he ever got engaged to her? And what about Moyra's child anyway? She *couldn't* have been telling the truth. Or could she? Perhaps she had lost hers too - like Lorne.

She paused, out of breath and totally confused. In spite of all her protests to the contrary, being pregnant was taking it out of Lorne. Worse still, nobody knew anything about her predicament except for Dr Garcia and Lilly.

Lorne breathed in to calm herself as Morton came running towards her.

"Lorne, Lorne, have you seen Dad? I want him to take me out on the water. Boardsailing." Lilly must have said something to Lance because Lorne had found out that he'd been the model father and spent hours with Morton teaching him how, on the smallest board he could find.

Morton loved the water and it was all she or Lilly could do to keep him out of it. He was utterly fearless but, unfortunately, it was a dangerous coast. There had been several drownings since Lorne had arrived. And two of them had been locals.

But, although the sea looked rough far out there were a few young men on their boards still braving the waves, making towards the pointed, rocky headland.

"He won't be coming down yet, Morton. He's playing golf with someone."

That *someone* was Shane.

The little boy looked very disappointed but, like his father, his mood changed very quickly.

Next moment, he was dragging at Lorne's arms which were aching already. "Don't, Morton. Here, carry this for me." She handed him her pretty holdall, containing

122

her towel and everything else a girl needed for serious sunbathing. Although that was the last thing she felt like. The sun kept giving her a headache.

"Okay." Morton lugged it gamely along. Then he looked up at her with the cheeky gap-toothed grin. "You'll have to come in with me, Lorne."

"No. I'm too tired."

"Gee, it's Saturday. And you've been doing nothing all morning." It was quite true. Suddenly, Lorne felt cross with herself. She was getting to be a bore. She had to pull herself together. After all, according to the doctors, pregnancy wasn't an illness.

"We'll see, Morton, but I'm not promising."

"Granma, Granma." Morton was shrieking already as he pulled her bag along the sand. "Lorne says she'll take me boardsailing."

Lilly had taken off her sunglasses and was patting the lounger next to her. "Hush up, Morton, Lorne looks as if she needs a rest. Now you go play in the sand while she and I have a chat. Go on now."

Morton dumped the bag and ran off. Next moment he was plumping down on the sand and digging into it furiously with his spade.

"Good, that's settled him for a bit. Now . . ." Lilly scrutinised Lorne's face, "I think what you need is to lie back and forget everything. I'll keep my eye on that little mischief."

"You're so good to me, Lilly," said Lorne, "but I really will have to try. I have to feel better soon."

"Of course you will. And then you can start making some decisions."

"Decisions?"

"Yes, about coming clean to the young man who got you in this position. It's partly his responsibility. It takes

123

two to tango and I know if I was in his shoes, I'd want to." Lilly could be extremely forceful at times. What she said was the truth of course - but it wasn't that simple.

"Of course I want to but . . ."

"You're scared?"

"I suppose I am."

"Well, you think about it. You can't go on like this." Lilly put on her sunglasses again and stared determinedly at her knitting. Lilly was right. She couldn't. Being a one-parent family seemed like a nightmare just now. How would she manage? It wasn't like Lorne to feel so miserable. She supposed it was her hormones.

She lay back in her chair and let the sun warm her legs. She didn't feel like being in the full heat just now. She closed her eyes and listened to the clicking of Lilly's needles against the sound of the waves, her mind flicking back to the past and then on to her present predicament. She wondered exactly how long her usually-flat tummy was going to last as she locked her hands across her as though she was self-conscious in her swimsuit already.

"Lorne? Why are you asleep? Don't you want to go in. I want to." Morton's voice was insistent. "I know how to boardsail. Dad showed me."

Lorne opened her eyes and looked into his pleading green eyes, then at the gappy heart-jerking smile. She couldn't blame Morton for looking like Lance. It must be no fun for the little boy playing alone all the time.

She pulled herself together. "What exactly do you want to do, Morton?" she asked. His eyes sparkled. He knew he was near winning.

"See my board? I only want to go in. Not too far. All you have to do is watch me close. I wanna show you what I've learned. How I can stand up." The board and its sail were coloured phosphorescent green and pink and, although it was smaller than the usual, the apparatus still looked daunting,

"Are you sure you can stand up on it?" smiled Lorne.

"You just come and see," argued Morton. Like his father, he had a way of getting what he set his heart on. Lorne sighed.

"Okay then, but not for long. It's too hot."

"It won't be in the water." That was true. Lorne looked at the waves warily. They were choppy, but it wouldn't do any harm just staying near the shore.

"What are you up to now, pest?" asked Lilly.

"Lorne's going to take me in." Morton was jumping around excitedly.

"Are you?" asked Lilly, putting her sun glasses up on to her grey hair again and glancing sharply at Lorne.

"Not far, I can tell you. I'm feeling better now actually."

"I don't think that cold water will do you much good." Lorne grimaced at the words.

"Well, I won't go in deep. I'll just watch him."

"Is it safe?" asked Lilly. Lorne squinted across the bay. The big rollers were a long way out. It must be. The wind wasn't that strong either, although it had evidently blown the other young windsurfers to their destination round the point.

"I should think so. Anyway, we won't be far from the edge. We'll be fine." She nodded to convince herself. "Come on then." With a bright wave to Lilly, she and Morton, who was grinning with delight, began to drag the sail board towards the ink-blue waves. . .

* * *

Lance and his passenger didn't have much to say to each other as they travelled fast through the open countryside in the limo in the direction of the coast. The American flicked a tiny sand fly off his immaculate white golf trousers.

He glanced at Westonman. Perfectly turned out. Suave - but you could still tell the guy was English in spite of his Italian clothes. He had that aristocratic look about him which informed the world he thought he was some superior being.

They'd played a round of golf which Lance had won and they'd talked business, said all they had to say. In fact, Lance could tell the guy didn't have his mind on the game. He was probably thinking how to pull a fast one. No way. But, now it was all up to the Englishman.

Lance planned to pick up Morton and his mother from the beach before he took Shane on to dinner. The kid's presence might soften up Westonman and remind him there were other things in the world instead of just business. And there was Lorne.

He was sure Lorne would be there too by now and he had a gut feeling that Shane Westonman was more likely to be extra responsive when his beautiful assistant was present. Lance hadn't missed the way Westonman looked at her. And Lorne was an asset which needed using to best advantage. But he hoped she was on the ball. She'd been looking real peaky since he'd proposed and she'd turned him down. But he was confident he'd get the right answer in the end, whatever his mother said. He didn't believe a word about her being in love with some mythical English guy.

"Sure hope you don't mind me making a detour. Pick up my kid from the beach."

"Sounds reasonable." Shane lifted a dark eyebrow. Probably kids were beneath his notice Lance thought.

He still wasn't sure where he stood with Westonman.

126

The guy never let anything slip and it seemed he wasn't willing to show his hand until Lance firmed up the figures. He drove a hard bargain but he was a shrewd businessman and he was fully aware how much was at stake, Lance concluded. A complex like Lance was planning was worth millions of dollars. Shane wasn't going to let the deal slip. No way.

The limousine, driven by Juan, made its way along the coast road. On each side, the barren landscape was only alleviated by a white cottage here and there or, occasionally, a gathering of flats and houses built in the African style, looking like honeycombs with arched windows.

"The whole island looks like a building site," said Shane suddenly.

"Yep, great isn't it?" replied Lance. Shane looked at him sharply. He was thinking about how green and beautiful the Cornish countryside was when he left it.

"At least the coast itself is more picturesque," he added shortly. Lance shrugged. He could see nothing wrong with the place. The island was ripe for development.

"The Costa's okay. My kid's down there all the time. I'm teaching him to boardsail."

"Really?"

"The little guy's fearless," boasted Lance. "Down here!" he ordered. Juan turned the car right, on to the road that ran above the beach, and cruised along. Lance leaned forward and stared through the smoked glass windows, his quick eyes searching for the familiar Denver logo on Lilly and Morton's brightly-coloured umbrellas.

Just as he spotted them he noticed people running excitedly along the beach and crowding on the water's edge. There was something up.

"Slow down, Juan. Open the windows." They slid down with a hiss and next moment, both men were squinting into the sun, which gave the heaving waves the colour of molten silver . . .

* * *

The sea was very cold and Lorne shivered as she went in with the waves breaking over her legs. Morton laughed and laughed, splashing her annoyingly, and struggling to tow his short sailboard behind him.

She turned away. "Stop splashing me, Morton. Please. I'll get used to it in a minute. Then I'll help you" She didn't think she would. The cold seemed to strike right up through her stomach. An eerie feeling gripped her. What if it did something to the baby? Would she care? But, suddenly, she knew the answer to that.

Being extra brave, Lorne bent and scooped the water over her, shuddering. It was the only way to stop Morton fooling about and driving her crazy. So she ducked her shoulders under, splashing water all over herself. A few seconds later, her body was zinging and warm.

"Come on then," she challenged. Morton was still struggling with the board and not making much progress. "Okay, I'll help you."

Soon Lorne and Morton were pushing and pulling the pretty small board deeper into the surf, further into the rollers, the sea now up to Lorne's waist with the much smaller Morton already swimming, his legs making frog-like motions. "Great, isn't it?" The little boy jerked his head towards the board.

"Yes, it's nice," she agreed, looking down at Morton and his board. The cold feeling had gone away and she was enjoying herself. Not thinking of the mess she was in, only about what she was doing right that minute.

Lorne shook her wet hair out of her eyes and blinked

at the board's bright white green and pink colours, sparkling in the sun, throwing off a sheet of dazzling light.

"It's brand new. High-density foam with a plastic shell." The little boy spluttered as the water went into his mouth. He was like a little fish himself, darting about, scrambling and leaping up and down on the board. Lorne laughed at him showing-off. Morton looked so much like Lance at his most arrogant.

"Why are you grinning like that? I know all about sailboarding. Dad taught me." He was trying to clamber on to the board again.

"I wasn't really laughing at you, Morton."

"Okay then." The little boy cheered up. Next moment, he and Lorne were in deeper water, forcing her to swim, while Morton, still trying to climb on the board, was slipping and squealing all the time.

And then he was astride and starting to put up the sails. "See what they're for, Lorne? They're semi-rigid. That gives a better thrust in the wind."

"Really?" spluttered Lorne, holding on to the board. A wave had just covered her head and filled her nose and mouth with water. It was at that moment she realised the ocean wasn't as calm as it looked from the beach. And the wind was getting stronger. "Morton," she shouted, "I don't think this is a very good idea. We're getting too far out." He didn't hear. She shouted again. "Morton, it's too rough." He heard that.

"No, it isn't," he shouted back stubbornly. "Once I'm up on my feet, it'll be okay."

"No, I'm going to tow you back," replied Lorne, grasping at the board.

Suddenly, Morton had managed it, was standing up and hanging on to the rigging. The wind caught the sail and spun him right out of Lorne's grasp. In just a few seconds, there was a distance of meters between them.

"No, Morton, come back now. It's too rough," Lorne screamed into the wind. She could feel the water swirling under her legs and that buoyant feeling you get as you swim deep. It was all she could do to breast the waves but her only thought then was that they were already too far out and she should have taken more care. And Morton was being blown further and further away.

It was a horrible moment like in a movie when you know something terrible is going to happen. As Lorne glimpsed the gaily-painted board whizzing away, she heard Morton shout. In a haze of streaming sea water, she saw the little boy topple backwards into the sea, striking his head on the board as he went down and under. Next moment the sailboard was turning over, and its pretty sails disappeared, engulfed in the trough of an enormous wave.

Lorne was struck with one moment of panic. There was no sign of Morton's orange life jacket. Where was he? Oh, no. . . He must be underneath. Trapped. She'd have to dive for him.

Without a thought for her own safety, Lorne began to strike out frantically in his direction, towards the spot where Morton had disappeared.

Back on shore, people had noticed what was happening and were running to the water's edge. . .

* * *

"Say, what's going on out there?" asked Lance as the car stopped.

"I don't know but I'm going to take a look," replied Shane. Next moment, followed by Lance, he was out of the limo and leaping down the steps to the beach . . .

Lilly Denver ran screaming towards her son. "Oh, thank God, you're here, Lance. It's Morton and Lorne. They're out there . . ." Clutching at her chest, her face grey-white, she was pointing towards the ocean. "Something's happened. The sailboard turned over."

"What? Lorne?" Shane's voice was husky with running. He stared at the plump woman as she gesticulated frantically, his quick eyes and brain taking in the terrifying situation.

And Lance was gripping her arm.

"You mean it's Morton. Out there." Next moment, he was throwing off his jacket and shirt. But Shane had beaten him to it. The Englishman was already heading for the water's edge and was running madly into the foaming waves.

Lilly was clutching at her son. "Don't be a fool, Lance, you'll be drowned. They've called out the launch." But Lance took no notice. He was staring at Shane already swimming strongly in the direction of the white speck which was the sailboard's upturned bottom. "Damn, damn, damn!" With a horrified look in his eyes, Lance let his mother's trembling body go and headed off as well, wading first then throwing himself into the surf.

"My son. My grandson!" Then a white-faced Lilly Denver collapsed on the beach to be surrounded immediately by a group of concerned onlookers.

Lorne was terrified that Morton was trapped under the sailboard; that he'd injured himself when he fell; that, somewhere, down in the inky-darkness of the ocean water, the little boy was struggling for his life.

The thought was enough. She had to find him. Drawing a great gulp of air into her lungs, Lorne dived under the water into the darkness. She could see nothing, no one, once the white shape of the sailboard disappeared. All she could feel was a strong current dragging her down from the ankles.

As she fought against its strength with an almost superhuman effort, a terrified Lorne realised that the current must have sucked Morton in and carried him away.. Its evil grasp was pulling her down too; the last glimmer of light from the surface seemed to be getting farther away. Down and down . . .

Lorne's body felt very, very cold; weightless; powerless against the current but she'd never been one to give up. She found she was determined to survive. She felt her lungs bursting and made an heroic attempt to strike for the surface again. She knew she must remain calm and swim across the current if she could. It was hopeless to fight against it.

Summoning all her strength, she began to strike across and upwards using a long, slow stroke; all the time trying to push away the feeling she was choking; but it was no use. . . The current was starting to win.

Then she knew she had to have the strength. A new thought fixed itself in her mind. She *had* to save herself and the child she was carrying. *Shane's baby*. If she drowned, it would too. And no one would ever know how it had lived warm and safe inside her. If she gave up now . . . Her arms pointed upwards mechanically, Lorne reached and stretched for the surface and air. . . Her legs and feet kicked her on and up . . .She had to live. She had to.

Shane had swum in rough seas before. He had been a sea-swimmer all his life and those years living near the wild Cornish coast were now paying off. He was drawing nearer and nearer to the little sailboard, striking out with a fast crawling motion.

But he was experienced and wary. There was probably a current. *That's why he couldn't see any sign of life.* But the waves were big. Maybe they were hidden? Shane fought off the cold feeling that he might be too late.

As the current began to tug at his heels, he swam on across it deliberately, towards the overturned sailboard. And, as his head turned from side to side, he was conscious suddenly of a flash off to his right; appearing orange against the white board, bobbing up and down. *It must have surfaced suddenly. Thank God*, he thought, *she's wearing a life jacket.*

But, then, he realised that the life jacket belonged not to Lorne but to a small child, who was floating, face upwards, in the water. As Shane reached him, he could see the young boy's face, white and still. There was a large bruise on the side, extending to his temple. He was unconscious. But there was no sign of Lorne.

Shane grabbed hold of the boy. He couldn't do anything for him now, except get him to shore. But what about Lorne? He couldn't leave while there was a chance she was still alive. He looked about frantically. Where should he dive? What could he do? Where had she gone? Under the board? Or yards away from it?

Clutching the boy's jacket in one hand, Shane grabbed for the sailboard, giving himself time to catch a breath. The boy must have been knocked unconscious when he fell off. . .

Just as Shane was deciding what course to take, about ten meters away he suddenly glimpsed white. His heart lurched as he realised that someone or something was very near to the surface. Letting go of the boy in the life jacket, who would go on floating - Shane struck out for the spot.

A few moments later, he was diving under the waves,

his eyes blindly searching; begging and praying to himself that what he had seen was not just a piece of wood or debris.

Then the thud of a body hit his and he flung out one arm and grabbed at it. Next moment, he had hold and was pulling it back up to the surface. As they met light and air, Shane's horrified eyes seemed to encompass the whole bizarre scene in a fraction of a second; Lorne's blonde hair floating out helplessly like some eerie sea anemone, her pure white body motionless, milky, under the surface.

He didn't know if she lived, only that it was a miracle she'd been able even to reach the surface given the force of the current. Was she alive? He wasn't sure. Unspoken thoughts froze his brain, terrible implications, numbing him with fear. In that sudden frantic fight against death seconds ago, the thought he might have lost her had never crossed his mind until now.

What would he do if Lorne was dead? Shaking the water out of his eyes, Shane set his teeth. If he could only get her back to the boy and the board, they could hang on until help came. . . Tiredness was pulling at him, weakening his strokes. With his eyes fixed on the bobbing orange spot which was Morton Denver, a struggling Shane called on the last reserves of his strength and towed Lorne towards him and the sailboard.

When he was almost there, he realised there was someone else in the water too. Lance had made it to his son, was holding on to him and the board, exhaustedly treading water, looking round like a madman. Shane shouted, "Start towing him in, man. For God's sake, get a move on. I've got Lorne." It was then both men heard the sound of the motor launch making its way to the accident spot.

Eyes closed, they clung on to each other, hung on

134

while, all the time, the greedy current cheated out of its prize, tried to drag them under. But, soon, lifebelts were being thrown into the water and Lance and Shane, together with the men on the boat, were hoisting up the unconscious bodies of Morton and Lorne.

As the launch turned and headed back to the shore where an ambulance stood at the top of the steps to the beach, sirens blaring, Shane was straddled over Lorne, with Lance watching dully, huddled and shocked like a dead man, clutching his son to him.

Shane had her head tilted back and was pinching her nostrils with his thumb and forefinger. Then he took a deep breath and blew steadily into her mouth, his dark eyes dilating with anxiety as he watched to see if her chest would rise.

"Come on, Lorne, come on, my darling, you can make it," he muttered gruffly, eyes full of tears, as he paused every five seconds to recoup his breath and pour it into hers.

Her response to his kiss was agonisingly slow but, finally, he was able to sit back, clutching a blanket about him, chafing her hands in his, watching her laboured breathing as the life flickered back into her body.

It was then that he looked up to the smiling blue sky and thanked God he hadn't lost Lorne after all.

* * *

135

CHAPTER 9

The pristine white paint and the characteristic clinical smell of the room turned Shane's churning stomach for the hundredth time. He couldn't stand hospitals but had always considered them a necessary evil. Now, for the first time in his life, he knew personally he was glad they existed.

He lifted his head off the pillow. It was a nonsense he was there at all; but they'd insisted. He admitted he was dog-tired.

The efforts both he and Lance Denver had made in that life-saving rescue attempt had been enough to land both of them a night in the hospital clinic, but he and Denver had insisted in not being admitted formally until they'd been given the news that Lorne and the child were out of danger. Now, a couple of hours later, Lance was in the next room with his son and Shane was lying turning over in his mind everything that had happened . . .

What it would be like to have a kid? To be a father? He'd never considered it since Moyra had done the dirty on him. Just put the thought clean out of his mind. His anger at being naive enough to believe her had dissolved, but it still hurt a hell of a lot.

Sometimes, it was like a deep place inside, which he kept bottled but occasionally the bitterness overflowed.

The only way he could bear those times was to shove them away - out of his mind. To put the whole damn disaster down to experience. Shane had vowed he'd have nothing to do with children after the trick Moyra played on him.

He hadn't always felt like that. With Lorne now . . . it might have been different. When he'd been with her, it had crossed his mind that one day they might . . . but she'd run off, hadn't she? Never gave him a chance to explain.

He didn't blame her for it. Anyway, how *could* he have explained about Moyra's so-called *predicament*? Lorne would never have wanted to see him again anyway. So he'd been stupid enough to play the gentleman. It was only after Lorne had gone, that he knew he missed her desperately; how much she meant to him.

Then there'd been the shock of finding her again. Working for Denver. And it was because of missing her, he hadn't been able to control himself that night when he'd come to her flat. He'd wanted to tell her about the present situation between him and Moyra but he'd chickened out. He'd really believed it was better he left.

In fact, he'd lost his nerve. He was okay in the boardroom but he was a shit where emotions were concerned.

Shane clenched his fists. He'd really done it again, hadn't he? Now she still didn't want to know him. He was a bloody fool. He turned over and over in the bed restlessly.

He didn't want to think about all this now. It was enough for him to know she was out of danger. As soon as he was out of the bed and she was well enough, he'd be there at her side and, maybe, he could get some things straight with her; things that had been bugging him for God knows how long.

Yes, Shane concluded, finally turning on to his back, his dark head resting on his long arms. It had been something to see Denver's look when the man had been told the kid had come round, *it was quite a thing having a child.*

Naturally, like every man, and woman he supposed, the idea of leaving something behind, attracted him. A part of oneself. And, when he'd seen Denver's face, it had struck him what it would be like to almost lose one. But Morton had survived.

Denver's mother had said it was something to do with the kid's body temperature dropping. A miracle that there was no brain damage either from the blow or the fact he'd been under the water too long before his life jacket had brought him up to the surface.

Shane was glad for Denver and for himself. Maybe there was a chance he could still square things with Lorne. He had asked the doctor to keep him posted.

Lilly Denver had been really helpful. In fact, she seemed to have Lorne's interests at heart. Evidently, Lorne confided in her.

Still, thought Shane, *not surprising given how keen Denver is on Lorne.* He didn't like the thought. But he'd seen them together, hadn't he? Maybe Shane didn't have a chance with her any more but he'd like to get things straight. Lilly had filled him in on the fact that Lorne's own doctor was looking after her here. That she was in good hands. Yes, Lilly was a nice lady.

Evidently Dr Garcia manned the clinic on some days and when the accident happened he'd been on duty. The clinic was a small outfit not like the casualty departments back home. But it was certainly efficient.

Shane glanced round and sighed. Well, he'd be out in the morning but he wasn't going to sleep until he'd had

138

a report on Lorne. He rang his bell for the nurse. But it was the doctor who turned up.

Dr Garcia looked down at the man in the bed. He was strong as a horse and wasn't going to suffer any ill effects from his ordeal. He'd acted the hero as well as Denver. It had been a foolhardy enterprise. They could all have been drowned and Garcia had seen plenty of deaths from drowning on this coast.

But, given it was Lance's son involved, what was this man's interest in Lorne. Garcia could see that the Englishman had been nearly out of his mind with worry. The doctor hadn't taken long to put two and two together. But he had to be careful.

"How is she now?" Shane's face was white and strained.

"Lorne is much much better. Both she and the boy have been very lucky indeed. Thanks to you and his father."

"Thank God. And when can I see her?"

"She's asleep now but, as far as I can see, she's got off lightly. She's a fit girl. Ethically, I should be giving this kind of information only to close relatives. However, as Lorne is a long way from home and you evidently saved her life, I can't see the harm in it." He knew he was right now. This must be the father. But did he know?

The first sensible words Lorne had said to Dr Garcia had been to ask whether she'd lost the baby. But she hadn't - yet. And it looked, if things went well in the next few hours, that wasn't going to happen now. But, there was always a chance of miscarriage given her history . . .

"Have her parents been told?"

"Yes, Lilly Denver has been in touch. They're coming over. You know them, Mr Westonman?"

"No, we've never met but, doctor," Shane bit his lip,

"you might have guessed that Lorne means a hell of a lot to me and I'm grateful for you keeping me informed."

"That's okay."

"And you're sure there's no permanent damage?"

"None that we can tell. Of course, her lungs took a beating but, as I said, she's fit. Anyway, I'm sure she'd like to talk to you. And thank you."

"There'll be no need for that," replied Shane. "I did what anyone would do."

"And more, I think. No, not anyone, Mr Westonman. You put your life on the line and that's always something special." The doctor patted his arm. "And, if I may say this, I think it will do Lorne a lot of good, if you tell her that she means a *hell of a lot* to you." He grinned. "Night then. See you tomorrow. Have a good rest. You deserve it."

Funny bloke, thought Shane, watching him go. *In England, you'd never get a doctor saying something so emotional. But the Spanish. Well!*

Shane yawned. Yes, he was damn tired and it was about time he took the doctor's advice. He turned over and, in a couple of minutes, he'd dropped off to sleep.

* * *

"I think you should tell him," said Lilly. "About the baby."

She'd been a very early visitor. Lorne was propped up in bed and stared back weakly. "What do you mean?"

"I think you should tell that young man who galloped off into the sea to rescue you - without a thought for himself in his head. Shane. It's his, isn't it?"

"Yes," said Lorne after a few seconds silence. "Yes, it is - but I don't think I can." There was a break in her voice.

Next moment, Lilly was sitting on the bed, her arms round her. "Of course you can. You have to. He cares about you. I can tell that."

"How? How can you tell that, Lilly?" Lorne's eyes were full of tears.

"By everything he said. By his face. His looks when Garcia told him you were going to be okay. If ever I saw a man in love, it's him."

"In love? Shane in love with me?"

"Of course he's in love with you. So why can't you tell him?"

"Oh, Lilly, if only you knew. But I can't, I can't. It's not that simple." Lilly held her shaking shoulders.

"Now, now honey, don't upset yourself. It won't do either of you any good - and you don't want to lose the baby now, do you. Not after you've held on to it all through that dreadful accident."

"No, no, I don't." Lorne was beside herself.

"Do you want to tell me? Can I help?"

"No, not now. Please, Lilly, I'm sorry, but not now. I have to think this one through. Please?"

"Sure. That's fine but, if you need a shoulder to cry on - or laugh for that matter, I'm here. You know that. But, listen to an old woman who's seen a thing or two. That young man *cares* about you. Okay?"

"Okay." Lorne nodded her head and scrubbed away her tears. . .

* * *

Shane's heart lurched when he saw how beautiful she looked. But so fragile. With a pang, he remembered how her hair had floated out like a sea anemone's and how her pale, slim body had looked under the

141

water. Then the ghastly feeling when he'd thought she was dead.

"Hi," he said. "How are you?"

"Hi. I'm okay now - thanks to you." He wanted to rush to her, hold her in his arms, keep her close so that nothing terrible could happen to her again. Keep her safe. But he just stood there, like a stranger.

"Come in. Don't stand at the door." Her eyes took in how pale he looked, the set of his mouth and the strain in his expression. But when he smiled a hot wave of feeling ran through the whole of her body.

"I'd have brought you flowers but I didn't have time."

"Don't be silly." He sat down beside the bed. She swallowed at his nearness, thinking of being in his arms; of telling him everything; how she carried his child; how her one thought had been to save it. Everything. But the words wouldn't come.

"Lorne, I know - I've been . . ." he faltered. She'd never seen Shane Westonman at a loss for anything.

"Shh, it's okay." Her fingers brushed a wisp of hair back from her eyes. "But thank you anyway."

"For what?" He was burning with shame and guilt inside.

"For saving my life, of course - and Morton's."

"His Dad did that. But I'm glad I was around - for you." He stared at her. She was so pale. "But, you don't look too good." His eyes were searching her face. "You look like you lost weight."

"Well, that's always a good thing," she lied.

"Look, Lorne," he stared down at the bedclothes, then up again into her eyes, "I *have* to say something. To explain. About that night I came to the flat - and - *left*. . ."

"You don't have to. It's over now." Inside, Lorne was raging. Even though she felt totally, utterly drained, she wanted to catch hold of him, scream at him what

142

he'd done, hold on to him, but she couldn't do a thing - until she knew the truth why he'd walked out on her - about him and Moyra. . .

She felt faint at the thought. Unreal. Lilly's words threaded through her mind. Anyone could see the man loves you. Did he? Did he? Then why the hell couldn't he come out with it and say so? Why was he still with that woman?

A sharp pain stabbed her inside. She gasped.

"Please don't get upset, Lorne, I don't want to upset you, but I don't know where to begin. I've made too many mistakes. . ." His voice seemed to be coming from far away. That old dizzy feeling was sweeping through her. She felt sick. But she knew she couldn't faint while she was lying down. Or could she?

He put out his hand and took hers. It felt very cold. His sharp eyes searched her face. There was sweat on her forehead. This couldn't be right and the doctor had said she was okay.

"What's the matter, Lorne? What's happening? Darling, what's happening?"

It didn't even register he'd called her *darling*. She couldn't think of anything but the pain again. Panic hit Shane as she fell back against the pillow, her face twisted with pain.

"Oh, Shane, no!" she gasped, clinging to his hand. "Shane, ring for the nurse." He leaped out of the chair and pressed the red emergency button. The buzzer flashed with an urgent bleeping. Next moment, as he felt her hand slip from his, he was racing across to the door and shouting down the corridor.

"Quick, get in here. Quick." Next moment, he was back by Lorne's side until his place was taken by a running Dr Garcia and two nurses.

A horrified Shane stood back as the doctor bent over his patient, oblivious to everything except what was happening. "Blood. She's bleeding," he said curtly. "Right, let's get going on this. She's losing the baby."

Shane's Spanish wasn't that good. He heard the words in a daze; then grabbed hold of Garcia's arm as he straightened.

"What's the matter, doc? What's happening?"

"I'm afraid Lorne is pregnant. And she is losing her baby."

"What?" Garcia saw the look on his face.

"And, now, we have to do something about it. . ."

It was like a bad dream. Next moment, Shane's eyes followed Lorne as she was hurriedly wheeled out of the room on a trolley accompanied by the medical team. . .

Lorne was having a baby - and she was losing it. . . He couldn't believe it. He just couldn't. . . Shane leaned back against the door and closed his eyes. Then, next moment, he was racing down the corridor behind them. . .

* * *

"Do you think they'll let me in now?" he asked Lilly.

"I hope so," replied Lance's mother anxiously. She glanced at his white face. "I'm sorry, Shane. But I told her she should tell you."

"You knew then? Tell me what?"

"Oh, dear, it isn't my place but - someone has to say it. It is your baby, Shane. She told me."

His mind was working over time. It must have been that wonderful, awful, night at the flat. And she'd never said a word. All the signs had been there and his pride had kept him from speaking to her, saying anything.

144

"I didn't know. I thought . . ."

"You mean you thought someone else was in the running?" He nodded. "No, dear, no one else. My son tried but, no, I'm afraid that Lorne had you fixed right there." Lilly Denver pointed to her chest. "I don't know the ins and outs of your relationship with her but she's one hell of a girl. And I think you have to go in and tell her that. Especially now."

He had the same kind of amazed look on his face when Lilly told Lorne that she was sure Shane loved her. They were like a couple of children. But, well, what were they? Early twenties? Lilly sighed. They had an awful lot to learn - and a long way to go. . . At that moment, Dr Garcia appeared. And he was smiling.

"Is she going to be okay?" Dr Garcia glanced from his strained face to Lilly's.

"Yes. The crisis is over. They are both going to be fine, as far as I can tell."

"Can I see her?" Shane was on his feet and staring at the door.

"Yes, but - don't upset her."

"I won't. I promise." The doctor nodded. Next moment, Shane had slipped into Lorne's room.

* * *

He just held her. He was going to hold her safe for the rest of their lives. He knew that now and explanations could come later. And she was going along with it too. Lorne could feel his heart beating quickly close to hers. She closed her eyes. This was where she wanted to be. This is what she wanted to remember. None of the bad times. Why he'd done what he'd done, didn't seem to matter any more. They could sort it out. This time was different,

145

her woman's instinct told her. She could trust him. Implicitly.

"Are you pleased about the baby?"

"My darling, I've never been so pleased about anything in the whole of my life - except, of course, finding you again."

She nestled into his shoulder. "And Moyra?" she whispered.

"That was all a terrible mistake. I never loved her. It was always you. She lied to me. She said that she was . . ." he stopped. He couldn't tell Lorne that Moyra had said she was pregnant with his child. He would afterwards, but not now. Nothing must upset her the doctor said.

Lorne lifted her head. "I know what she said, Shane. She came and told me you were getting married. That's why - I ran away."

"Oh, love, I'm so sorry." He kissed her and she clung to him. "It wasn't true."

"I know."

"I wanted to tell you that night at the flat but - I - was afraid."

"You were afraid?" She couldn't imagine him being afraid of anything. "So was I." She looked into his eyes. "Afraid that you'd gone away and would never come back. Afraid to tell you about our baby in case you thought . . . oh, I've been such a fool."

"No, it was me who was the fool. Letting you go." He felt love, desire, every emotion for the girl in his arms; for the mother of his child; and it was really his child this time. . .

Lorne let him hold her and caress her. His touch and only his was what she yearned for. All she'd wanted. Ever. *Forever yours, Shane, darling*, she whispered in her heart. And this baby was safe. Later on, she might tell him about the other.

"Are you happy, Shane?" she whispered.

"Yes. Are you?"

"Yes." He hugged her gently.

"Then we'll be happy ever after," he said. And that was all Lorne had ever wanted to hear him say.

THE   END

Also available in the

MYSTERIES OF THE HEART

series

Tides of Love - Helen McCabe
The Sands of Time - Liberty Brett
After the Rain - Aisling Byrne

Helen McCabe

Tides of Love

Could Fran's childhood sweetheart, Declan O'Neill, have
been responsible for her father's mysterious death at sea?

One stormy night, Fran is prepared to risk everything to
find out. Even her own life, and that of the man she loves.

ISBN 0-9525404-2-8

Liberty Brett

The Sands of Time

What was the mystery surrounding Rik Fenton? Pippa
had to fly to Cairo to find out; a trip which led her into
deadly danger. But she was determined to unravel the
secret.

ISBN 0-9525404-3-6

AISLING BYRNE

AFTER THE RAIN

Should ex-Army officer Alison trust Richard? What was the secret he was keeping from her? Could the Army be to blame again?

ISBN 0-9525404-7-9

**Also available from Peacock Publishing Ltd
in the SPLENDOUR series**

Two for a Lie - Helen McCabe
Eve's Daughter - Michael Taylor
Raven's Mill - Helen McCabe

Forthcoming Title - Spring 1998

A Driving Passion - Michael Taylor

Eve's Daughter

Michael Taylor

'A fascinating read. This highly enjoyable novel conveys vividly the flavour of life at the turn of the century.'
The Rt. Hon. Dr. John Gilbert, MP.

Lizzie Bishop, full of romantic dreams, finds fulfilment when she marries Ben Kite. But two former rivals for her affection, Stanley Dando, her enigmatic second cousin, and Jesse Clancey, the likeable and handsome son of a prosperous neighbour, remain secretly in love with her. Then Ben, with the noblest of intentions, makes the biggest mistake of his life, and everybody is caught up in the spiralling consequences.

Sensual, riveting, poignantly tender, and often hilariously funny, Eve's Daughter draws the reader into an enthralling saga of obsessive desire and deceit. Set in a Black Country community in the early 20th century, the characters are engaging and vividly true to life. A brilliant debut novel.

'Michael Taylor comes into that small group of male writers able to achieve a warm empathy with the heroine.'
Dr. Hilary Johnson.

'From the first sentence it grips your attention . . . an absorbing read.'
Leigh Rowley - The Dudley News

ISBN 0-9525404-5-2

Helen McCabe

Raven's
Mill

'Helen McCabe has done it again! Well researched; believable characters and a chillingly realistic villain.'
Sue Sallis.

Beautiful Lydia Annesley returns to Upwych from London at the age of eighteen to take her rightful place as heiress to a salt fortune. To her dismay, she discovers that handsome, brooding Caleb Vyne, who is both her business rival and the master of sinister Raven's Mill, appears to have other ideas. Lydia soon finds out to her cost, what price she has to pay for her beauty, her fortune, and her business.

This tender and passionate love story, set against an authentic background of the Victorian salt industry, draws the reader into the world of powerful brinemasters grappling for total supremacy. But feisty heroine, Lydia Annesley, can hold her own in both love and the salt business. The unusual background for this novel makes for both an exciting and rewarding read.

'. . . a terrific novel. I enjoyed its dramatic intensity and the historical backdrop very much. . .'
Victoria Evans, Carlton UK

ISBN 0-9525404-1-X

A DRIVING PASSION

Michael Taylor

Lovely Henzey Kite is wary of allowing herself to fall in love again after her first heady affair with prosperous man-about-town, Billy Witts. But men find her beauty and her talent as an artist irresistible. Then, deeply drawn to handsome engineer Will Parish, a widower, Henzey finds another man vying for her love; wealthy motor manufacturer Dudley Worthington, a married man. Only Dudley is aware of the astonishing links between these three men; links that are enough to turn all their lives upside-down. . .

Set within the external glamour and internal graft of the burgeoning West Midlands' motor industry in the 20s and 30s, *A Driving Passion* is a spellbinding saga of obsession, agonising love and restless guilt.

A sequel to *Eve's Daughter*, this compulsive tale confirms Michael Taylor as one of the few male writers able to achieve a warm empathy with the heroine.

Due out Spring 1998

ISBN 0-9525404-6-0

All Peacock books are available at your local bookshop. In case of difficulty, they can be obtained from:

Littlehampton Book Services Ltd.,
10-14 Eldon Way
Lineside Industrial Estate
Littlehampton
West Sussex BN17 7HE
United Kingdom

Direct Sales Line:
01903 736736 (fax no. 01903 730828)
International +44 1903 736736 (International fax +44 1903 730828)
Please quote the title you require, author, ISBN, and credit card number - Visa/MasterCard.

Card No._____

Expiry Date _____

Signature_____

Peacock Publishing Ltd. reserves the right to charge new retail prices, if necessary, which may differ from those shown.

Title_____ Quantity_____

Author_____ISBN_____

Address to which book(s) to be forwarded:

Name_____

Address_____

_____

Please allow 28 days for delivery